"Clar[e] ... give you a commitment—not right now. It's up to you whether this goes any further,"* Kelly said.

She stood thinking for a moment, but she knew she had already decided to take what she could have of Kelly McGinnis.

Her silence was driving him crazy. He had to know what she wanted. "Talk to me, Clare. Tell me to get out of your life, or—"

"All right." She spoke with a sureness she didn't feel. "No commitments for now. Shall we shake on it?"

He scrambled out of his chair, nearly knocking it over, and grabbed her shoulders. His mouth was rough as he took hers, almost violent in his need. For a man who was getting what he wanted, there was a desperate quality in the way he held her, as if he wanted to imprint her on his body, as if she'd vanish in a wisp of smoke if he let her go.

Finally he pulled away from her. "Are you sure this is what you want?" he asked.

She reached up to bring his mouth back to hers. "You couldn't have come into my life at a worse time," she whispered against his lips, "but I've never wanted a man like this, as though my insides are falling apart and you're the only person who can put me back together. . . ."

WHAT ARE *LOVESWEPT* ROMANCES?

They are stories of true romance and touching emotion. We believe those two very important ingredients are constants in our highly sensual and very believable stories in the *LOVESWEPT* line. Our goal is to give you, the reader, stories of consistently high quality that may sometimes make you laugh, sometimes make you cry, but are always fresh and creative and contain many delightful surprises within their pages.

Most romance fans read an enormous number of books. Those they truly love, they keep. Others may be traded with friends and soon forgotten. We hope that each *LOVESWEPT* romance will be a treasure—a "keeper." We will always try to publish

LOVE STORIES YOU'LL NEVER FORGET
BY AUTHORS YOU'LL ALWAYS REMEMBER

The Editors

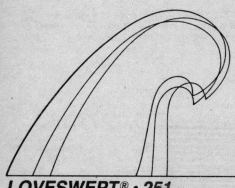

LOVESWEPT® • 251

Patt Bucheister
The Luck of the Irish

BANTAM BOOKS
TORONTO • NEW YORK • LONDON • SYDNEY • AUCKLAND

THE LUCK OF THE IRISH

A Bantam Book / April 1988

LOVESWEPT® and the wave device are registered
trademarks of Bantam Books. Registered in U.S. Patent
and Trademark Office and elsewhere.

If you would be interested in receiving protective vinyl
covers for your Loveswept books, please write to this address
for information:

Loveswept
Bantam Books
P.O. Box 985
Hicksville, NY 11802

ISBN 0-553-21890-5

Published simultaneously in the United States and Canada

Bantam Books are published by Bantam Books, a division
of Bantam Doubleday Dell Publishing Group, Inc. Its trademark, consisting of the words "Bantam Books" and the
portrayal of a rooster, is Registered in U.S. Patent and
Trademark Office and in other countries. Marca Registrada.
Bantam Books, 666 Fifth Avenue, New York, New York 10103.

PRINTED IN THE UNITED STATES OF AMERICA

O   0 9 8 7 6 5 4 3 2 1

Good times . . .
   Good friends . . .
      Good health to you . . .
And the luck of the Irish
   In all that you do!

One

Kelly McGinnis wondered if he could be getting senile at the ripe old age of thirty-five. He was certainly acting strange.

For the third Wednesday in a row he was seated at a table in a restaurant staring out the window at a fashionable boutique across the street. He wasn't interested in the elegant clothing worn by the anemic mannequins in the display window. He wasn't acting that strange.

He and his sister had a standing date for lunch each week. When he had told her several days ago to meet him at the same restaurant for the third week running, she had protested. And he hadn't been the least bit surprised. The restaurant was hardly distinguished. The food wasn't particularly good, the service resembled a snail's Sunday stroll, and its location was inconvenient for both him and Megan. Still, without any explanation, even though he knew she was expecting one, he insisted they eat there.

If he told Megan it was because he wanted a glimpse of a woman he didn't even know, she would immediately demand a family conference to have his black-haired Irish head examined.

Kelly's deep blue eyes narrowed as he stared at the entrance of Chez Madeleine across the street, irritated that the mysterious woman who had been haunting him still hadn't arrived. Shaking his head in self-disgust, he decided his sister would be justified in calling in the head doctors. To be obsessed by a woman he didn't know was definitely certifiable.

He had first noticed his mystery lady three weeks ago when he had happened to look out the window while lunching with Megan. For some unexplainable reason he couldn't look away. He watched her get out of a gray limousine, her slender figure elegantly dressed in an ivory silk suit with a gray fur stole casually draped over one arm. About twenty minutes later, he saw her come back out of the boutique wearing faded jeans, a light blue sweater, and a tan jacket of questionable vintage. The limousine had driven off after she had entered the store and she didn't appear to be looking for its return. She walked away from the shop and disappeared around the corner. That first day he barely managed to restrain himself from chasing after her, realizing it would be the foolish action of a berserk man, namely Kelly Neil Michael McGinnis.

He couldn't pin down exactly what it was about her that had caught his attention. It wasn't that she was stunningly beautiful, although she wouldn't win an ugly contest, at least he didn't think so, judging from what he could see of her features at a distance. Her figure was neither voluptuous nor scrawny. Perhaps it was the graceful way she moved that stirred his imagination, making him think of soft music, moonlit nights, and hot sheets. Maybe it was the mystery.

Maybe he was nuts.

She arrived looking like a queen and left looking like a pauper. She apparently never bought anything at the boutique. The only thing she carried was an oversized bag slung over her shoulder. It would make more sense if she went in wearing jeans and came out elegantly dressed, not the other way around. She could have arranged to have her purchases delivered, but that didn't explain why she came out of the boutique in inexpensive everyday clothes nor why the limo didn't wait for her.

The second time he saw her, she had followed the same pattern and now he was just waiting to see if she would show up again this Wednesday.

He glanced at his watch. She was late.

But Megan wasn't. A hand on his shoulder and familiar "Hi, Kel" brought his attention away from the window to the dark-haired woman who brushed past him and slid into the plastic-covered booth across from him. It was the same booth they had shared the week before. He got the same raised eyebrow he got last week. He disliked booths. Megan knew that he preferred a good chair at a wide table, but the booth was next to the window with the straight shot view to the boutique, so he had to sit there.

Megan examined her elder brother's face as though she might find in his expression the reason for his odd behavior. All she saw was the same face she had known all her life. Thick black hair, tanned skin, laugh lines radiating from the corners of slate-blue eyes, and a subtly aggressive jaw. If his strong mouth didn't curve into a smile as often as it used to and he no longer teased her unmercifully, it was due to painful experiences with divorce. Otherwise he looked the same, a bit preoccupied with staring out the window at the moment but basically the brother she had known all her life.

Megan pried his attention back to her. "Yoo-hoo! Remember me? Your little sister?"

Kelly tore his attention away from the window. "Sorry. Hi, Meg. How are you?"

"Peachy keen, thank you, and hungry. I don't understand why you keep insisting we have lunch at this oregano palace. Every time I go back to the office, my secretary makes comments about eau de garlic."

His gaze wandered back to the window and the boutique entrance. "There's something I need to check on near here." There was still no sign of the gray limousine. He turned away from the view and he gave his sister a rueful smile. Coming to his senses at last, he promised, "This is the last time. Next week we'll have lunch wherever you want."

Megan settled back against the booth and picked up the oversized menu. "I'll be a good sport as long as this is definitely our farewell appearance here."

The waitress took her sweet time with other customers before getting around to Kelly and Megan, so they had ample opportunity to catch up on family news and each other's lives. Megan and Kelly were the only two unmarried members of the family, both having tried marriage and failed. There was only a year between them and they had always been close, but they were even closer now that they had suffered similar endings to their marriages. The pressures put on them by members of their large family to try to work things out instead of divorcing had bonded them together even more. Out of seven children, Kelly and Megan were the only ones who had unsuccessful marriages and no children, neither fact going down well with their parents.

Although Kelly loved Megan dearly, she had one

fault that drove him crazy. It didn't take long for her irksome trait to surface.

"Kelly, there's someone I'd like you to meet."

His head snapped around and he glared at her. "Not again," he said, clearly exasperated with her. "I wish you would stop throwing women at me, Megan. I'm perfectly capable of getting a date if I want one."

"Oh, pooh," she said scathingly. "I've seen some of those women you've taken out. Their chest measurements are bigger than their IQs." She grinned as he glowered at her, holding her hand up in a placating gesture. "I'm not pushing Clare at you, although I think you should take her out. You could do a lot worse, you know. She needs—"

"Megan, I don't care what she needs," he interrupted rudely. "She'll have to fulfill her needs with some other jerk. It won't be me."

"I was going to say," she went on patiently, "that she needs some advice on renovating an old house she's living in. This is strictly business. I thought of you when she mentioned wanting expert advice. Really, Kelly. You seem to think I have nothing better to do than to plan your personal life."

"You've been giving it a damn good try."

"I have not."

"Yes, you have. You do it all the time."

"I do not."

Two Irish tempers were off and running. And while they were intent on squabbling, the gray limo pulled up in front of Chez Madeleine.

Clare Denham felt as though the weight of the world was on her shoulders as she pushed open the glass door and entered the rarified atmosphere of the fashionable boutique. Going to the nursing home dressed in borrowed finery always depressed her, but it was something she had to do. Her gray high-heeled shoes sank into the plush carpet as she walked toward the back of the shop. No matter how many times she told herself she was doing the right thing, she still hated the deception she carried out every Wednesday.

Madeleine was in her office. Clare stood in the doorway balancing while she removed first one shoe then the other. "Hi, Maddie."

Lifting her elegantly coiffured blonde head, Madeleine Bronski grinned. "How did it go today?"

Clare entered the office and set the shoes on the shiny surface of the desk. Taking one of the white chairs near the desk, Clare began unbuttoning the suit jacket. "Mrs. Hamilton's condition is about the same. I tried again to get her room changed to one that didn't look out onto the street. I'd like to be able to eliminate the expense of the limousine, but there's nothing wrong with Mrs. Hamilton's eyesight. She'd spot me getting out of my old Mustang and wonder why I was driving such a disreputable automobile. She sighed. "I should never have rented the limo that first day. Now she expects it."

"How long do you think you can keep up this charade?"

Folding the suit jacket carefully, Clare took a deep breath. "As long as I have to. I'd better get out of this outfit. I'm always so afraid I'll get a spot on these clothes."

"I told you not to worry about them, Clare. The clothes I lend you are the ones we've had on the mannequins. They have to be cleaned before they go on the sale rack anyway. Besides, as you know, I outfit the two women newscasters at the local television station in exchange for free advertising. This place is a regular lending library of clothes."

Clare smiled at her friend's bored tone of voice.

Maddie made light of the favor she was doing, and Clare knew her friend wouldn't want any gushing show of gratitude.

"I hate fooling Mrs. Hamilton like this, but it gives her pleasure to think I'm doing well with the studio."

"You *are* doing well. If you didn't pour all the profits from the salon into that nursing home and Mrs. Hamilton's medical expenses, you could afford to *buy* these clothes."

Standing up, Clare grinned. "I don't need your expensive clothes anyway, except for an hour or two every Wednesday."

Crossing one silk-clad leg over the other, Maggie commented, "You'd have plenty of opportunity to wear my fancy clothes if you'd go out with my lawyer's partner. How many times has he asked you? And you refuse every time."

Clare headed for the door. "Excuse me, Maddie, but I've heard this routine before. I have to change. I'm supposed to meet someone at the restaurant across the street."

"A man?" Maddie asked hopefully.

In the doorway, Clare looked back over her shoulder, shaking her head in exasperation. "You have a one-track mind, Maddie. No, I'm not meeting a man. The last thing I need right now is a man cluttering up my life."

"But *dahling*," Maddie purred in a mock sultry voice. "Men are such adorable clutter."

Laughing, Clare went into one of the fitting rooms to change into her own clothes. Maddie loved the male of the species and made no bones about it, but spent more evenings at home than out on the town. Clare knew she was more talk than action. In the two years she had known Maddie, Clare had never known her to go out with a man more than twice. She preferred to play the field, but she was choosy about who she played with.

Meeting her reflection in the full-length mirror, Clare smiled at the amused expression in her eyes. At least Maddie had a field to play and the time to play it.

Shrugging, Clare let her gaze slide down the pleated white satin blouse tucked into tan slacks, and adjusted the slim gold belt at her waist. She slipped her arms into a brown blazer and stared critically at her overall appearance. This outfit was a bit of a comedown from the silk suit she had just taken off, but it was all hers and she was definitely more comfortable wearing it.

A few minutes later the transformation was completed to her satisfaction. She had brushed out her hair and removed her makeup except for a light touch of eyeliner and mascara. The rest of the week she had to wear perfect makeup and immaculate hairstyles. On her days off and on Sundays, she preferred to look natural without the powder and paint she sold in the salon.

A darting glance at her watch had her gathering up her purse. A few minutes later she left the boutique and headed for the restaurant across the street. She was ten minutes late.

The hostess was escorting an elderly couple to a table so Clare looked around the crowded restaurant to try to find the person she was supposed to meet. She spotted Megan, and then noticed a man sitting across from her. He must be the carpenter Megan had mentioned. Clare hadn't realized Megan was bringing him along today.

Weaving around the tables, Clare went toward the booth. The man's back was to her, but Megan was facing her, although she was too engrossed in talking to the black-haired man to pay attention to anyone around her. When she'd taken a few more steps, she realized that talking wasn't the proper word. Megan was flat-out arguing.

She was several feet away when she heard the man ask, "Don't you know anyone who can get a man on her own? I'm getting tired of you flinging all these old maids at me."

Clare stopped, not particularly anxious to step into the middle of an argument. She decided she had been wrong. He didn't sound much like a carpenter. Their conversation sounded private. She waited to hear Megan's reply. She didn't have long to wait.

With flashing eyes, Megan replied, "Contrary to your exalted opinion of yourself, there are women who are more interested in the work you do than your body. Clare is one of them."

Clare's eyes widened. He had been talking about her! Old maid indeed. If he was the carpenter Megan recommended, the blasted man could take his trusty hammer, his saw, too, and sit on them.

She took a step forward and heard him remark, "I wish we could have lunch just once without you bringing up some girl you've met who you think would be perfect for me, Megan. When you start bringing them with you is when we stop these weekly dates."

Megan quickly looked down at the table, suddenly very interested in the silverware, her expression changing from angry to guilty.

Leaning his arms on the table, Kelly drawled threateningly, "You didn't."

"It's not what you're thinking, Kelly. I told you, it's business."

"Sure. Of course it is. One of your looney sex-starved cronies from the office is going to plop her skinny buns down next to me and tell me how she needs my services."

Just then Megan noticed Clare standing behind Kelly.

Megan's aghast expression would have been funny under other circumstances, Clare realized. Unfortunately, she was too furious to find the situation amusing.

When Kelly saw his sister's face, he frowned and turned to see what Megan was staring at in horror.

Slowly he turned his head and met tawny eyes, tiger's eyes, blazing golden eyes that took his breath away. His shock at seeing the lady from the limo so close kept him speechless. Having a fantasy appear before him was a stunning event. His imagination had not done her justice. All he had to do was reach out and he would be able to touch her, which was tempting—except for the piercing look in her eyes. She didn't seem as happy to see him as he was to see her.

Moving forward, Clare held out her right hand toward him. "Hi. I'm skinny buns."

Megan's burst of laughter didn't help much. Kelly groaned and slumped against the back of the booth. This wasn't the way he had hoped to meet his mystery lady. Since faint heart never won fair lady, though, he extended his hand and clasped hers, feeling the instant current of awareness flow through him. "Hi, I'm wrong."

Clare gave him a blank look. "What?"

"I'm wrong. You don't have skinny buns. It's too early in our relationship to know if you're sex-starved."

Smiling sweetly, Clare commented, "Since some very nice men in pretty white coats will be coming along to take you back to your room at the home for dingdongs, you'll never know, will you?"

He might be crazy as a coot, but Clare discovered she liked the sound of his rich laughter and the way his eyes glittered with amusement, lines of humor crinkling at the corners of his eyes.

Still holding onto her hand, he tugged her toward him, sliding over to make room for her when she was forced to sit down beside him. He kept possession of her hand, resting their clasped hands on his hard thigh as he glared at his sister who was chuckling, thoroughly enjoying the predicament her brother's mouth had gotten him into.

"Megan, if you could control your warped sense of humor for a few seconds, I'd appreciate an introduction."

Still grinning broadly, Megan carried out his instructions. "Clare Denham, the smooth-talking son-of-a-gun on your right is my brother, Kelly McGinnis."

Clare's expression was slightly wary as she looked at the man who still held her hand. "How do you do, Mr. McGinnis?" She paused for a moment as she tried to pull her hand away from his, but her resistance only made his fingers tighten, pressing hers into the hard muscle of his thigh.

Pleased that her voice sounded so cool, considering her heart was racing uncomfortably from the current of charged energy shooting up her arm, she asked, "May I have my hand back, Mr. McGinnis?"

"Is it important to you?"

She met his gaze squarely, not backing down from the challenge in his eyes. "Well, I came with it. I'd kind of like to leave with it."

He was no longer amused. His fingers tightened almost painfully around hers. "You're not leaving? You just got here."

Clare had no opportunity to answer. A waitress with an astonishing abundance of bright orange hair piled haphazardly on top of her head approached their table with a pad and pen poised to take their order. She aimed an expectant look in Megan's direction and wrote down her order for a salad and linguine.

The waitress's heavily mascaraed eyes flicked to Clare next, a hairpin falling out of her hair when she moved her head.

Clare looked down at her hand still captured on Kelly's thigh, then glanced up at the man beside her who showed no sign of releasing his grip on her. She then looked over at Megan, who had a blank expression on her face. She was on her own. Weighing her options, she knew she could make a scene about getting her hand back, but she had a feeling this Kelly McGinnis would enjoy it and still get his way.

With a resigned sigh, she murmured, "I'll have a chef's salad."

The waitress's sculptured eyebrow lifted in inquiry when she leveled her gaze on Kelly. If she looked longer at the dark-haired man than she had at his companions, few women would have blamed her. His features weren't classically handsome like her favorite movie star, Tyrone Power, but he filled out his blue shirt just as nicely and the lazy, amused expression in his blue eyes made her wish she was twenty, oh, all right, thirty years younger and forty pounds thinner.

Kelly gave the waitress a smile that could melt a spinster's iron reserve and told her he would try the lasagna. Her pen scratched across the pad automatically without her once looking at the surface she was writing on. She only looked away when Kelly shifted his attention to the woman next to him.

After the waitress finally sauntered away, Kelly released Clare's hand, satisfied she would stay long enough to eat her lunch. He planned to use the time to learn more about the woman who had occupied his thoughts during the last three weeks.

"Megan said you wanted to meet me," he said casually.

Her eyes widened in surprise as she stared at him briefly before slanting a glance at Megan. "Exactly when did I say that?"

Megan's eyes were bright with amusement. "When you asked if I knew anyone who could give you an estimate on the renovations you want done on your house. I do know someone." Her head nodded in the direction of her brother. "He's it."

"*You* are a carpenter?" Clare asked.

"I prefer the term 'woodwright,' " he clarified.

"Really? Why is that?"

His smile indicated he had expected her bewilderment. "My company specializes in custom woodworking. We build or restore moldings, hand-hewn beams, paneling, carved custom trim, that sort of thing."

"I see. Doing all those things makes you a woodwright and not a carpenter?"

"I like to think so. Carpenters build the foundation of the structure. My craftsmen add the decorative icing on the cake."

Remembering the rough texture of his hand, she asked, "Do you do any of the actual . . . ah, woodwrighting yourself?"

Smiling, he replied, "As much as I can. I have more administration to attend to than I like but I try to work with the other artisans whenever possible."

His sister felt compelled to add, "Kel's also had a book published on colonial woodworking tools and techniques and has several apprentices he's teaching the methods of a colonial woodworker."

"I'm impressed," stated Clare, meaning it. "How does one become a woodwright?"

"I spent four years working in Colonial Williamsburg as an apprentice while I was attending William and Mary College. I discovered I liked working with my hands."

"I noticed," she said dryly, referring to the way he had taken possession of her hand earlier.

"There's a lot to be said for using one's hands," he drawled lazily. "To touch, to stroke, to feel the shape of the object. I like to run my hands over smooth, satiny surfaces."

The air around them crackled with a sudden electricity as he gazed intently into the tawny depths of her startled eyes. Clare's flesh tingled as though he had been stroking her skin instead of the wood he had been talking about. Or was he talking about wood? Her hand still felt the imprint of his fingers and she rubbed it with her other one to try to erase the sensation his touch had caused.

"A man should love his work," she murmured.

"And women should too, of course," Megan contributed.

"And women should too," conceded Kelly, not wanting to get involved in one of Megan's feminist lectures. He had heard them all before. Now he wanted to hear about Clare Denham. "Do you love your work, Clare?"

She shrugged. "I like my work. I wouldn't go so far as to say I love it."

Wondering if her occupation was the reason for her transformation from princess to pauper, he asked, "Exactly what do you do?"

Megan answered for her. "She makes magic."

It was Kelly's turn to look bewildered. "You're a magician?"

Clare's "No" coincided with Megan's "Yes." Kelly's confusion grew. Looking from one to the other, he asked with bewilderment in his voice, "Which is it? Yes or no?"

Giving Megan an amused smile, Clare supplied the explanation. "I'm a cosmetologist."

After a short thoughtful pause, Kelly drawled, "And you had problems with woodwright?" Shifting his hips slightly on the seat, he used her earlier phrasing. "How does one become a cosmetologist?"

His thigh was now pressing against hers but she didn't change her position. Whether he did it on purpose or not, she wasn't about to give him the impression that the feel of it bothered her one way or the other. Because it didn't. Not one bit.

She met his challenging look and answered his question. "One gets a degree in cosmetology."

A corner of his mouth curved up. "And then what does one do with a degree in cosmetology?"

"One hangs it in one's office in a salon where one helps beautify the female population."

With a wry grin, Megan added, "And a few males."

Kelly had some answers but not enough. Flicking a glance out the window at the boutique across the street, he realized he was no closer to finding out about her unusual Wednesday performance than before. Bringing his gaze back to the woman who had occupied his thoughts so much during the last three weeks, he attempted to dig a little deeper.

"Do you travel around with a case of goopy stuff as well as work in a salon?"

The waitress approached and while their lunch was being served, Clare answered his question. "It's a little more complicated than being an Avon lady, Mr. McGinnis."

"Would you stop with the Mr. McGinnisses? My name is Kelly."

Picking up her fork, Megan began to regale Kelly

with more information regarding the world of cosmetology, in between bites of linguine. Kelly's face took on a rather dazed expression as her explanation included such things as facials, waxing, the various use of creams, emollients, and powders. His sister finished by stating, "It's similar to the work you do, Kelly."

His dark skeptical brow rose. "I think the garlic fumes are getting to you, Megan. I work with wood."

"You both start with something basic and make it more attractive. The surfaces are different but the premise is the same. You both use your specialized skills to recreate and emphasize the natural beauty of the original object." She gave them each a smug smile, very pleased with herself. "You have a lot in common, which is why I wanted you to meet each other."

Recalling the remark she had overheard Kelly make earlier about his sister meddling in his life, Clare looked at him. Her frown matched his.

Kelly caught her expression and read it correctly. Clare didn't like being manipulated any more than he did. Megan was lunging ahead as usual without thinking. If he was ever going to get to know Clare better, he had to have a chance to change her initial impression, which hadn't been greatly enhanced by his well-meaning but bungling sister.

Looking directly at his sister, he asked softly, "Megan, aren't you going to be late getting back to your office?"

Megan's blue eyes widened in astonishment and then changed to a look of comprehension. She was the boss and no one could possibly complain if she was late, but it finally dawned on her that her brother wanted her to leave.

Glancing at her watch, she exclaimed with exaggerated horror, "My gosh, is that the time? I really have to run." Gathering up her purse, she quickly slid out of the booth, telling Clare she would call her later at the salon. Then with a wink and a wiggle of her fingers in her brother's direction, she exited like the tail end of a whirlwind.

Clare slowly folded her napkin, her thoughts on Megan's startlingly fast exit. The reason behind it was about as subtle as a matador's suit of lights. Irritated, she placed the napkin beside her plate. She needed a carpenter, not a blind date.

"I must be going too. I have things to do."

Kelly's hand clamped down on her arm. "What's your rush? You haven't finished your lunch."

"Neither did Megan but you didn't try to stop her from leaving."

"I didn't want her to stay."

Surprised at his frankness, Clare looked at him warily. "I don't know what you and your sister have cooked up between you but I—"

Interrupting, Kelly drawled, "My sister does the cooking and the stirring up. Occasionally she boils over and everyone within shouting range feels the heat, but she means well." His fingers loosened a little around her arm but not enough for her to pull away from him. He went on. "Megan can be a royal pain in the posterior at times but she doesn't mean any harm. She has one glaring fault though. She's like an Irish Noah. Feels everyone should travel in twos."

"I don't need a matchmaker. I need a carpenter."

He leaned back against the booth, releasing her arm. "So tell me about this house you want renovated."

A small smile curved her lips and drew his gaze to her mouth. "I don't need a woodwright. I need a carpenter."

"Let me be the judge of what you need," he said quietly, an odd note in his voice. "Is there major structural damage or is it only minor repairs?"

Since he was discussing business, she relaxed. "I don't know. That's why I need a carpenter or a contractor to come out to the house and check it over. I can see some obvious repairs, like several loose rails on the staircase. There are a few windows with wood rot. A couple of shutters were damaged in a storm. There may be more problems that I can't see. I need an estimate so I know how much money I'll have to—" Quickly changing the direction of her statement, she said, "How much it will cost. The original owner kept the house in good condition while she was living there but for the last two years Mrs. Hamilton has been ill and unable to take care of the house. It's my responsibility now."

"Is the house yours or are you renting it?"

"Does that matter?"

"No, not really. It just seems that you're going through a lot of trouble and expense if it's not your house."

Clare felt his intent gaze on her face as she looked out the window instead of looking at him. "It's a little complicated," she replied evasively, knowing it wasn't an adequate answer. The whole situation with Mrs. Hamilton was difficult to explain to close friends. How could she expect a stranger to understand the obligation she felt toward the older woman?

The few people who knew of Mrs. Hamilton's present financial circumstances found it hard to believe the once shrewd businesswoman had lost the majority of her savings due to an investment decision made after she first became ill. The combination of medication and pain had left her confused and vulnerable, a dangerous time to evaluate and speculate on business matters.

Unfortunately, by the time she was feeling better, the damage to her savings had been done. With additional medical expenses and the cost of the long-term care in the nursing home, Mrs. Hamilton was in a precarious position financially for the first time in her life. And, because of the older woman's frail health, Clare kept the financial details from her. She had accepted the house and the salon from her elder friend only because refusing the gifts would have hurt Mrs. Hamilton. They had been the older woman's way of insuring Clare's financial security.

Now Clare had made the decision to sell the house to enable Mrs. Hamilton to receive the best medical care possible.

Kelly's gaze remained on Clare's face, noticing how her stunning eyes were suddenly shadowed with unpleasant thoughts. No, not unpleasant, he decided. More like bewildered, confused, sad, and unless he was mistaken, a little frightened. Protective feelings welled up inside him, startling him. He didn't even know her but she brought out emotions that surprised him . . . and tantalized him too.

A small plate with the bill on it was plunked down onto the table, bringing Clare's attention back to the restaurant and the man beside her. He was picking up the check.

Her fingers closed over the purse on her lap and she slid out of the booth. Lifting her chin, she took a deep breath and faced him. "I'll have to owe you for my lunch, Mr. McGinnis. I had planned only to have a cup of coffee with Megan and I didn't bring much cash with me. I'll give Megan the money I owe you when she comes to the salon for her next appointment."

What in hell was going on? he wondered. She shopped in an expensive boutique every Wednesday, and now was embarrassed because she didn't have the cash to pay for her meal. Apparently she didn't carry credit cards or she would have offered to use one to pay her bill.

He took in the proud tilt of her head. "This is my treat. Consider it my apology for the remarks you overheard."

She adjusted the strap of her purse. "Okay. Thanks." She turned toward the door and had taken several steps before she heard him call out, "Clare, wait!"

Looking back over her shoulder, she saw he had slid out of the booth and was tossing some cash onto the table. Several long strides brought him close to her and she had to tilt her head back in order to see his face. "Yes?"

He didn't want her to disappear again. He didn't want to wait until next Wednesday before he saw her again. Since he couldn't very well tell her that, he said, "We haven't set a time for me to look over your house."

A waitress balancing a heavy tray laden with steaming dishes scowled at them for blocking her way. Grasping her elbow, Kelly guided Clare around tables, waitresses, and other customers, drawing her toward the entrance of the restaurant.

There was no gray limousine parked anywhere near the restaurant that Kelly could see, so he directed her toward the parking lot at the side of the restaurant.

"We can decide on a time when it would be convenient for me to examine your house while I drive you home."

"I drove my own car."

She stopped by a ten-year-old Mustang and dug her keys out of her purse. After she unlocked the door, she turned toward him to thank him for lunch. She caught a look of astonishment on his face.

"What's wrong?"

His gaze roaming over the car, he asked, "This is your car?"

"Yes, it is." There was a slight edge in her voice when he asked defensively, "Why? What's wrong with it?"

It wasn't a limousine. That was what was wrong with it. What in hell was going on? One minute she tooled around in a luxurious limousine, dressed to the nines, and the next minute she drove this old heap. She was a cosmetologist with a large house she wanted to fix up, but apparently didn't have the money to pay for the renovations.

Compared to her, his grandmother who had talked to leprechauns was dull stuff.

Realizing he was taking a long time to answer her question, he replied, "There's nothing wrong with your car. I guess I expected you to drive something a little more—" He broke off, unable to come up with a word that wouldn't offend her.

"A little more modern?" Clare supplied helpfully. She patted the roof of her car affectionately. "Sadie has covered a lot of miles without giving me many problems. There's not a lot of people I can say the same for."

"Why do you call her Sadie?"

She shrugged. "Sadie just seemed appropriate somehow." Opening her car door, she hesitated and finally asked, "Were you serious about looking at the house?"

If it was the only way he could see her again, then he was dead serious. "Yes."

"I'll pay you for your time, naturally."

At first Kelly was going to tell her he didn't charge

for estimates, but he remembered the proud tilt to her head when she had been unable to offer to pay for lunch. She might misunderstand if he told her there wasn't a charge for an inspection. There was a better way to do it. He took one of his business cards from his wallet and handed it to her.

Accepting it, Clare saw his company's name and logo with the address and phone number printed on it. His name was in one corner and the words FREE ESTIMATES in bold type in the other corner.

Relief was evident in her eyes when she looked up at him. She hadn't known where she was going to find the money to pay him if he had charged for the estimate anyway. "When would you want to come out to the house?"

Kelly wanted to say *now*, but his instincts told him to go slow with this proud, complicated woman. "I have a few hours to spare late in the afternoon on Friday."

She extracted one of those plump organizer notebooks his secretary was so fond of, and he watched as she rifled through the pages until she found the section for March. Taking a small pen out of its holder in the center of the notebook, she asked, "Is four o'clock convenient?"

Smiling at her businesslike tone, he wondered what she would do if he pulled her into his arms and kissed her. "Four o'clock is fine. I'll need the address."

"The house is a little hard to find. Would you mind meeting me at the salon in the Beecher Mall around four? I'll drive you to the house or you can follow me there. You can get in touch with me at the number on this card if you can't make it."

He took the business card she handed him and slipped it into his shirt pocket. He wanted to do more than get in touch with her. His hands ached to touch her soft curves and silky skin. Instead, he imitated her businesslike tone. "I'll see you at four on Friday then."

He closed her door after she got in behind the wheel and stood beside the car. It took several attempts before the engine turned over and she was able to drive away. In her rearview mirror, she caught a glimpse of Kelly's tall frame still standing where she had left him, his gaze on the car.

Two

Kelly arrived at the Beecher Mall fifteen minutes
early. After looking up the location of the Beautique
Salon on the mall directory, he dodged kamikaze
mothers aiming strollers at his legs, and ignored the
various display booths situated in every available
space in the wide walkways. Clusters of people
blocked his way and children ran around as though
the mall was some gigantic playground. Shopping
malls were at the top of his list of places to avoid but
this was where Clare Denham was so this was where
he had to be. He would walk through fire in order to
get to her if he had to.

During the last couple of days, he had occasionally resented the hold Clare had over his thoughts
and his body. Even though the opportunity had
presented itself in the sultry shape of a more-than-
willing Miss Tanya Stanford yesterday, he had turned
down her invitation to stay after the other guests
had left the party. In fact he had arrived home at the
unheard-of hour of ten o'clock! Alone!

Somehow he had to exorcise Miss Denham from

his mind. He wanted no commitments, no permanent attachments, no long-term affairs, and no woman whose smile made him forget his distaste of all of the above.

The way he figured it, one night in his bed, well, maybe two, and Clare Denham would be just another name scratched out of his little black book.

The Beautique Salon was easy to find, but stepping into the carpeted interior was like stepping into a foreign land. Along one side of the spacious salon several women were seated at French Provincial vanity tables gazing into ornate mirrors while mysterious things were being done to their faces by attractive women wearing crisp white aprons trimmed in small dainty ruffles.

There were glass counters in the center of the salon with products displayed in a variety of ceramic, glass, crystal, brass, and copper containers.

"Can I help you?"

Kelly turned his head toward the softly modulated voice and saw a young woman seated at a small French Provincial desk at one side of the entrance.

Stepping over to the desk, he stated, "I have a four o'clock appointment with Miss Denham."

"Your name, please."

"Kelly McGinnis." Too late, Kelly realized the receptionist thought he was there for some sort of beauty treatment. He groaned inwardly, thankful his brothers weren't anywhere around or it would have been a long time before he would have lived this down. His brothers had extraordinarily long memories when it came to embarrassing moments.

The receptionist said politely, "One moment, please." She consulted a leather-bound appointment book in front of her, running a long varnished nail down a list under Clare's name. Even reading upside down, Kelly could see the straight line drawn down the middle of the column from four o'clock until the closing time of ten. Apparently, Clare had no further appointments for the day.

The receptionist glanced up. "Miss Denham has no appointment listed for four o'clock, Mr. McGinnis."

"Is she here?"

"Yes. She's in her office but—"

Giving the receptionist a slow smile, he suggested, "Why don't you tell her I'm here. It's personal, not professional."

Reaching for the white-and-gold phone on the corner of her desk, the receptionist depressed a button. A few seconds later, she announced his name into the phone and replaced the receiver.

"Miss Denham would like you to go to her office, please. It's the white door in the rear marked private."

Kelly didn't bother knocking. Clare was sitting behind an antique mahogany desk when he opened the door. This was the elegant woman who rode in limousines, not the one who drove an old clunker named Sadie. Her brown hair was coiled in an intricate twist behind her head, her tawny eyes accentuated expertly with several soft shades of flattering eye shadow.

Her voice was as rich and velvety as he remembered. "Sit down, Mr. McGinnis. I'm running a little late. Help yourself to some coffee," she invited, indicating a pot of coffee and some cups on a table against a wall. Gold bracelets clanked softly when she stretched out her hand.

Concentrating on the papers in front of her, she circled several items with a pen and then made a phone call. Kelly scowled, not because he minded waiting but because she still insisted on using his last name.

He poured himself a cup of coffee and took one of the chairs near the desk, relieved it wasn't one of those fancy spindly things he had seen in the salon. He looked around the office, taking in the plants, a watercolor painting on the wall behind Clare, the understated decor which was the opposite of the blatantly feminine trappings of the salon. He wondered which of the two reflected Clare's tastes. He liked to think she preferred her office. He did.

It was surprisingly difficult to keep her mind on the business she was supposed to be discussing on the phone with Kelly in her office. Maybe if she hadn't been thinking about him ever since she had met him, she wouldn't find his presence so disturbing. For about the hundredth time, she told herself to keep her mind on the problems she already had. She didn't need to get all moony-eyed over some man.

Just because he was the most compelling, irritating, attractive man she had ever met was not any reason for her to dwell on the way his eyes glittered with amusement, or to think about his lithe grace. But she remembered everything about him whether she wanted to or not.

In a few minutes, Clare hung up the phone and began to clear off her desk. Locking the middle drawer, she looked up to tell him she was ready to leave and stopped because of the expression on his face. "Why are you looking at me like that?"

He stalled. "Like what?"

"As though you've never seen me before."

"You look different from the way you did the other day. Extremely beautiful but untouchable. I like you better when you're mussed up a little."

Surprised changed quickly to amusement. "It's called gilding the lily. That's what we do here at Beautique. I can't very well walk around with no makeup and my hair flying every which way. Women don't trust experts who don't use the products they sell. It would be like going to a dentist who had decayed teeth."

He watched as she went to a cabinet and took out her purse, admiring the slender curves outlined by her svelte navy-blue dress. She came toward him, stopping a foot away from his chair. "We can leave now."

Kelly got to his feet and set his coffee cup on her desk. He slowly moved closer to her, reaching out to lightly touch the side of her face. "I've never touched a gilded lily before."

Her heartbeat thudded in her chest. Keeping her voice steady, she commented dryly, "I find that a little hard to believe. You don't go out with women who wear makeup? You don't touch them?"

A calloused finger followed the firm line of her jaw. Kelly didn't speak for a long moment, his attention on the silky skin under his finger.

Suddenly lifting his eyes to collide with hers, he murmured, "I don't remember any woman feeling this good."

He saw shock widen her eyes . . . and a brief flicker of something else in their golden depths, but it was gone before he could decide what it was.

She recovered quickly. "You don't appear to me to be the type of man who spends a lot of time alone, so you must have a short memory," she said tartly.

He knew he was going too fast for her so he smiled softly and said, "As much as I hate to argue with you on our first date, I—"

"This isn't a date!" She glared at him.

"Well, if you're going to get technical and insist our first date was lunch on Wednesday, then I stand corrected." His way of acknowledging her indignant intake of air was to deepen his smile. "Now about my memory. I want you to know I have an exceptional memory. I remember the birthday when my brother Daniel gave me a Captain Whizzo decoder ring. I can recall the time Mary Beth McGruder broke my nose. There was the visit to Ireland when I kissed the Blarney stone and—"

"That explains it."

"Explains what?"

Tilting her head to one side, she said, "Kissing the Blarney stone is supposed to give a person the skill to turn a flattering phrase, right? You're walking proof it works."

Kelly liked the way her eyes sparkled when she was trying to take him down a peg or two. She had had that same look when she threw the skinny-buns line back in his face last Wednesday. It did strange things to his equilibrium. "I heard that if you kiss someone who's kissed the Blarney stone, you'll believe anything an Irishman tells you."

"You made that up!"

He grinned down at her. "I'm willing to test the theory if you are," he drawled as he reached for her.

Clare moved swiftly away from his hands and to the door. She opened it. "I have a theory of my own. Do you want to hear it?"

He scowled at the distance she had put between them. "I don't think so, Lily."

She blinked in surprise at the name he had called her but went valiantly on. "I'll tell you anyway. My theory is if an Irishman doesn't follow a certain woman to her house, he won't know where she lives."

Kelly laughed. "An excellent theory. Not very romantic, but true." He started toward her, passed her, and stopped after he had taken several steps out of her office. He raised an arrogant eyebrow and asked, "Well, Lily? Are you coming or not?"

Several heads were turned in their direction, so Clare had to bite back the rude comment blistering her lips. Smiling sweetly, she shut the office door and followed him through the salon.

To make her disposition even worse, her car stalled twice at stop signs. Kelly's imposing black Blazer stayed complacently behind her, patiently waiting for Sadie to get her act together. The truck remained in her rearview mirror during the twenty-minute drive to Mrs. Hamilton's house. The turnoff from the highway was unmarked and partially hidden by bushes and trees. The one-lane road wound around several gentle curves, eventually ending at a white two-story frame house with a column-lined entrance.

Clare drove around to the side of the house while Kelly parked in front on the curved drive. After she had tucked Sadie into the garage, she came around to the front instead of entering through the side entrance off the garage as she usually did. Her plans were to show him around the house, pointing out the areas she thought needed work. Kelly was standing next to the Blazer, ignoring the slight breeze ruffling his dark hair, intent on the view.

The house was larger than he expected, but what claimed his attention were the fenced-in garden plots with neat rows of tilled soil ready to be planted in the spring. A small shed stood at one end of each plot. What in the world was going on? Was this her house or some sort of plant nursery?

His gaze took in all the surrounding grounds. At one side of a small white barn, there were two long greenhouses covered in heavy clear plastic. Through the plastic, Kelly could see blurred images of wooden tables laden with pots sprouting abundant green plants. Everything was neat and tidy, indicating someone spent a lot of time and effort to keep it that way. He didn't think that person was Clare. The hand he had held on Wednesday had been soft, free of the calluses she would have earned doing the physical work required to keep these grounds in such immaculate condition.

When Clare began to climb the steps toward the front door, Kelly called her back. She hesitated and frowned but did as he asked. Coming within several feet of him, she asked, "You can't see what has to be done to the house out here."

"Is all this yours?" he asked, his hand making a sweeping motion.

After a moment's hesitation, she answered, "Sort of."

"How can you 'sort of' own all this? Either you do or you don't."

"The property is in my name but I'm only sort of taking care of it for the original owner who isn't able to." She shrugged. "It's hard to explain."

There was that 'sort of' again. Gesturing to indicate the greenhouses and garden plots, he asked, "What's all this?"

"It's exactly what it looks like. Gardens and greenhouses."

"Let me rephrase the question. Why all this?"

Humoring him, she replied, "I've leased an acre of land near the barn to the Greensleeves Greenhouse. They constructed the temporary greenhouses and drilled a well. They will leave when their permanent facility is finished in town. The small sections of land are rented to residents of those new condominiums on Cunningham Street. Some of the people wanted gardens but they have no place so I rent them space out here."

A muscle in his jaw clenched. After a long moment, Kelly muttered, "Very enterprising."

Startled by his tone, she looked up, wondering why he sounded as though enterprising was a dirty word. His expression was unreadable so she gave up trying to figure out what he was thinking. Gazing out at the tilled land that had once been a large expanse of green grass, there was a trace of sadness in her voice as she commented, "I don't know how enterprising it is. I know it's necessary. It may also be necessary to sell the house which is why I want the repairs made."

What for? Kelly wondered. For money so she could ride in limos and shop in classy boutiques? Slanting a hard, vaguely disapproving look down at her, he asked, "To pay for the finer things in life? Scarlett O'Hara would undoubtedly approve. It's a shame to chop up this land though." He shifted his gaze to the pillared front of the stately house. "Anything to keep Tara, right? Except you don't want to keep Tara. You want to sell it to the highest bidder."

Clare absorbed the hurt his words caused, unable to understand why he disapproved so strongly. Lifting her chin defiantly, she turned away. It was none of his damn business what she did or why she did it. She hadn't brought him out here to judge her or the way she managed things. He could take his sanctimonious opinions back to town for all she cared. She marched to the front door and unlocked it. Inside, she tossed her purse onto the narrow hall table and turned when she heard Kelly's heavy footsteps behind her. So he had decided to continue with the job. Fine. One more crack, though, about Tara and he was in serious trouble. She might not be able to boast of an Irish temper but she had been known to singe a few male hides a time or two in her day.

Her heels tapped loudly in the wide hall as she walked over to the staircase. Rigidly, she pointed out the rails that needed replacing and waited in silence while he thoroughly checked each one.

She watched as Kelly bent down on one of the steps to get a closer look, the material of his dark slacks stretching tightly over his slim hips and thighs. Her eyes feasted, making a banquet of his masculine form. When his hand stroked one of the carved banisters, her skin felt a current of heat as though his callused hand were stroking her. She closed her eyes and concentrated on breathing normally, which wasn't as easy as it should have been.

Feeling ridiculous, Clare opened her eyes, angrily flailing herself for being a fool. The man was here to give her the benefit of his experience with wood, not to titillate her libido.

Running his hands over the varnished wood, Kelly was irritated with himself. He had been out of line spouting off about the way she ran the property. He had no right to criticize or condemn her for the way she managed her affairs. Her methods and her motives were none of his business. She apparently had her reasons and he was wrong to jump to hasty conclusions until he knew what they were. There were worse ways for a woman to make a buck.

The fury caused by his ex-wife's deceptions was still deeply embedded in his mind, and had caused his extreme reaction to learning Clare was doing what his ex-wife had done. But this time it wasn't his house or his life so he had no right to judge Clare. What was it about her that made him act like a rude opinionated rear end of a horse? That wasn't how he wanted to be with her.

Part of his frustration was there were too many inconsistencies in what he knew about Clare. Instead of getting to know her better, he was only finding more contradictions. She intrigued him as no other woman had, and he knew the mystery surrounding her was part of the attraction. He would be better off not knowing all the answers. After his divorce, he had vowed never to become emotionally involved or committed to any one woman again. It was safer to mind his own business. That's what he would do, he promised himself. He didn't need any entanglements with tawny-eyed women with skin like ivory satin.

Following her when she walked to another room, his body felt a surge of desire when his eyes couldn't resist the sight of her hips swaying gracefully with each step. Damn, he cursed himself. He should just try to take her to bed instead of attempting to analyze every damn thing about her. Making love to her would get rid of one of his frustrations.

Several times as he looked over the house, he caught himself thinking of renovations he would like to see done to the house but he forced himself to block out such thoughts. This house was just a job, nothing more. Getting personally interested in a building was something he had vowed never to do again.

He'd been down that road once before. Never again.

He was there to give her an estimate. That was all.

It took a little over an hour for Kelly to examine the whole house. There were five bedrooms and two baths upstairs, and a spacious living room, a dining room, a kitchen, and a book-lined study downstairs, along with a small bathroom off the downstairs hall. On the ground floor he found only the stair rails and two windowsills that needed any work, but upstairs, he noted several sections of molding that needed to be replaced and three windows which should be reframed.

One of those windows was in her bedroom. At least he guessed the room was hers. All the other bedrooms had dust covers draped over the furniture, the beds stripped of linen. Her room reflected the same taste as her office: warm, inviting, and comfortable. Her bed was antique mahogany and covered with an apricot-tinted duvet. The mahogany surface of her dresser gave a warm polished gleam from the light coming through the window. A chest of drawers against one wall had a single ornament on its shining top, a delicate porcelain statue. An extension phone and a small alarm clock were the only objects other than a lamp on one of the night stands. The one on the other side of the bed held a small green trailing vine in a copper container and a matching lamp.

His imagination ran rampant as he stared down at the bed, her bed, visualizing how her hair would look spread out on the pillow. The stirring in his lower body persuaded him to look somewhere else. Through a doorway he could see towels draped over one of the towel racks in the bathroom. His mind immediately conjured pictures of her stepping out of the shower and rubbing one of the towels over her arms, her breasts, her hips, her legs. He took a deep steadying breath to gain some control over his thoughts.

Snapping his notebook shut, he left her bedroom with long strides, relieved Clare had had the sense to retreat downstairs after showing him each room and leaving him to his work. He wasn't sure he would have been able to keep from reaching for her if she had been in the bedroom with him. Cursing his lack of self-control, Kelly took his time going down the stairs, giving his body a chance to cool down before he found Clare.

She heard his footsteps echo in the hall and knew he was looking for her. Seated at the table nestled in an alcove in the kitchen, she wrapped her hands around the mug of steaming coffee on the table in front of her. Unfamiliar with the way estimates were done, she didn't know if he was going to give her the results of his survey now or leave and send her an itemized list in the mail. She had set aside part of the money from the leasing of the gardens to pay for repairs. She only hoped it was enough.

Looking out the window at the woods behind the house, she heard him cross the varnished wood floor of the dining room. She continued to gaze out at the peaceful countryside when he pushed open the door. Steeling herself to face him, she turned her head slowly and met his quizzical gaze.

"Would you like a cup of coffee?"

"Sounds good." He came further into the kitchen and headed for the coffee pot. He heard the scrape of her chair and ordered, "Don't get up. I'll get it myself."

A few seconds later he pulled out the chair across from her and sat down. His small black notebook drew Clare's gaze when he set it down on the table beside his coffee cup.

"So what's the verdict?"

He caught the apprehension in her voice. "Considering the age of the house, it's in fairly good condition."

"So it doesn't need too many repairs?"

"I didn't say that, but there aren't as many as I expected to find in a house this old."

Looking around at the oak-beamed ceiling, where copper pans hung from a rack over a center worktable, she stated, "This house has been in Mrs. Hamilton's family ever since it was built almost a hundred years ago. She and her husband lived in it for years after her parents died and Mrs. Hamilton continued to live here after her husband passed away." Her eyes took on a faraway expression when she thought of the older woman who had loved this house. "This place was her pride and joy, the child she never had. Even with a large business to run and a large staff—a cook, a housekeeper, and two women who came in twice a week—she could be found dusting the furniture or polishing silver."

Since he hadn't seen anyone else in the house while he had been looking around, he thought he already knew the answer to his next question. "Where is the staff now?"

"They have found other positions." A soft self-conscious laugh escaped from her before she tagged on a brief explanation. "I'm not used to having household staff." Plus she couldn't afford their wages, but she didn't mention that.

"You can't possibly keep up this large house yourself."

Her eyes narrowed as though she were searching for signs of disapproval. She found only surprise and curiosity. "As you probably noticed, I don't use all of the house. I closed off a number of the rooms and covered the furniture. The rooms I do use I try to keep up in my spare time. This house is like a stately old lady. She deserves tender loving care and respect due to her long years of service to the family she housed. I don't have the heart to let her look anything but her best."

Kelly could remember feeling like that once about his own house, but he ruthlessly shoved the sentiment aside. The less he thought about the house he had loved, the better it was for his sanity. There was a harder edge to his voice than he had intended when he asked, "You're fond of the house, yet you are going to sell it?"

Pushing back her chair, Clare went over to the sink to rinse out her cup. "I'm fond of chocolate eclairs too but I do without them." Wiping her hands on a towel, she repeated her earlier question, "So what's the verdict?"

Instead of answering her question, he shoved back the sleeve of his jacket and glanced at his watch. "It's after six." Getting to his feet, he said, "Let's go out to get something to eat and we'll go over what has to be done to the house."

Folding the towel carefully, she took her time hanging it up. "Why can't you tell me now?"

"Because I'm hungry. I can't make rational judgments on an empty stomach." Going to the refrigerator, he opened the door and peered inside. "We certainly can't eat here. There isn't anything in your refrigerator but two grapefruits, an orange, and a peculiar green object wrapped in plastic that could either be a head of lettuce or something gone bad." He looked at her over his shoulder, a look of horror on his face. "You aren't a vegetarian, are you?"

She couldn't stop the smile that curved her mouth. Shaking her head, she replied, "I've been too busy to get groceries."

He straightened up and shut the door. "All the more reason to come with me. You need to eat some food more substantial than anything you have on hand." His eyes journeyed over her from her high heeled shoes to her ornate hairstyle. "But change first. We'll . . ." He suddenly frowned. "Why are you shaking your head? If you don't want to take the time to change, that's okay. I just thought you might be more comfortable in casual clothes."

"It isn't that. Is taking clients out to dinner standard practice?"

His smile faded. "You aren't a client yet, Lily. It's one of the things we have to discuss."

He was implying they had more to discuss than repair estimates but she didn't want to talk about anything but business with him. She was dangerously attracted to him and she didn't want to be. She would be stepping into unknown territory at a time when she couldn't stray from the course she had set for herself.

Kelly saw the indecision in her face. Even though he wanted to persuade her to come with him by taking her in his arms and convincing her, he stayed where he was. He decided to challenge her instead. "Are you afraid of me?"

As he expected, Clare's eyes flared with temper. "Don't be ridiculous! Of course not."

"Then spend a couple of hours with me. An hour. Only an hour. I'll give you all the information you want about the house while we have a decent meal. I don't know about you but I'm starving and I hate eating alone."

She had the sinking feeling his Irish charm was undermining her good sense. Sighing heavily, she agreed, "All right. One hour, one estimate, one dinner."

Kelly's smile held a hint of devilment that would put a leprechaun to shame. "At the risk of pushing my luck, could the hour start after you change into something that doesn't make you look like you just stepped out of *Vogue*? Do you have a pair of jeans?"

She didn't realize her mouth had dropped open until she tried to form words. "Why do you want me to wear jeans?" Her expression changed from puzzlement to one of suspicion. "Where do you plan to have dinner? I'll warn you right now, I'm not really excited about dining in treehouses or on horseback."

Laughing, Kelly took her arm and shoved her gently in the direction of the kitchen door. "I haven't decided where we'll eat yet but I promise it won't be in a treehouse or on a horse. I suggested jeans only because I wanted to see how you looked in them." He scooted her through the door. "Skip the jeans if you must but get a move on. I'm wasting away from starvation."

Muttering to herself about arrogant Irishmen, Clare stomped up the stairs. Fifteen minutes later, she came down a bit more calmly, dressed in aqua slacks with a matching textured short-sleeved sweater. Her sable hair waved softly around her face and onto her shoulders. When she had removed the pins to uncoil her hair, she had told herself she was only getting

more comfortable. Letting her hair down had absolutely nothing to do with a certain blue-eyed Irishman
who preferred her a little mussed.

Kelly wisely didn't comment on her changed appearance, although the warm glow in his eyes indicated he heartily approved.

Their first meeting had certainly been different.
So was their first evening together.

Kelly had been driving along the road toward the
city limits when a police car with blue lights flashing and strident siren blaring pulled Kelly over to
the side of the road.

Glancing quickly at Kelly, Clare didn't believe what
she saw. The silly man was grinning!

Instead of getting out of the patrol car to ask for
Kelly's driver's license, the patrolman pulled his car
alongside Kelly's and leaned over to roll down the
window.

Kelly rolled down his and called out, "Is it time?"

The policeman smiled widely and made a thumbs-up
gesture through the window. He yelled, "Follow me,"
and then sped away, his tires squealing. Before Clare
had a chance to ask Kelly what in sweet heaven was
going on, he had put the Blazer in gear and was
breaking the speed limit right behind the police car.

Clare didn't think it was terribly unreasonable to
ask what was going on but when she did, Kelly's
reply consisted of a brief apology.

"Sorry but we have to make a detour before dinner."

It never occurred to him to take her back home
first. Later he would wonder about that, but for now
he concentrated on following the police car.

The detour turned out to be the local hospital. If
someone he knew was ill, he certainly seemed happy
about it, she thought. After he had opened her door

he tugged her along beside him, catching up with the policeman as they neared the door. In the elevator, Kelly introduced the policeman as his brother Kevin and then immediately began asking questions about people named Devlin and Monica. Kevin replied that he didn't know anything except it was time. Clare was dying to ask time for what but the two men didn't give her a chance.

When the elevator doors opened, Clare caught a glimpse of a sign that read MATERNITY WARD as she was led toward the waiting room. The room was packed with black-haired, blue-eyed members of the McGinnis clan. By way of introduction, Kelly announced as all the heads turned in their direction, "This is Clare Denham," and then she was suddenly afloat in a sea of McGinnises. Her hand was shaken by people who introduced themselves in a confusing jumble of Seans, Bridgits, a Molly, one woman named Shelagh, a couple of Patricks and some others she couldn't remember.

She recognized a familiar face when Megan hailed her from across the room and waded through her assembled family to reach Clare. Kelly was pulled away by one of the other men and it was up to Megan to introduce their mother to Clare. Mary Kate McGinnis smiled at Clare, her blue eyes sparkling with good humor. She was a middle-aged woman with several gray streaks mixed in with the black hair gathered behind her head in a loose knot. The older woman's small frame fairly crackled with energy as she stood near Clare.

In a brogue as thick as her arm, Mary Kate McGinnis said, "A pleasure it is to meet you. So you've come with our Kelly, have ye now? Well, he'll be trying to calm our Devlin for a bit but never mind, you'll be as welcome as the robins in spring."

And she was. Even though Kelly and Megan were

the only familiar faces in the room, Clare didn't feel one bit out of place. Kelly's charming family wouldn't allow it.

From snatches of conversation, Clare gathered that "our Devlin" was the father of the next McGinnis about to enter the world. Since most of the men, including Kelly, were restlessly pacing the floor, she was unable to determine which of Kelly's brothers was the father-to-be. She did learn Kelly had four brothers, two sisters, an assortment of sisters-in-law, and one brother-in-law, along with an astonishing number of nieces and nephews.

She didn't even try to figure out who the various children belonged to. It didn't seem to matter. When one fell down, someone picked the child up. When one needed a hanky, the closest adult wiped the child's nose. Hugs and cuddles were given freely to whichever child looked like he or she needed or wanted one. All the children wore stickers which proclaimed they were guests of the hospital, passes handed out to them at the front desk with permission from the family doctor.

Clare couldn't help comparing Kelly's family with her own. The only child of workaholic parents, she had never had the automatic affection and closeness this remarkable family shared. Her parents were professional people, involved in their own separate work with little time to give to the daughter who had arrived in their lives unplanned and unwanted.

Each member of the McGinnis family was as excited by the impending arrival of a new member as though it was the most important event in their lives, dropping everything to be on hand to welcome the baby to the family.

Her own father hadn't even bothered to come to the hospital when she was born. That interesting fact had come out during one of the numerous quarrels between her parents that Clare overheard. Knowing her father didn't feel her birth was an important enough reason to leave his law office long enough to welcome her to the world had filled her with anger and hurt. He spent more time with the criminals he defended than he did with his own family. Her mother, also a lawyer, spent almost as much time away from home as her husband. It was left to a Japanese housekeeper to see that Clare was sent off to school and fed properly. No one provided for her needs for love and affection.

For many years, Clare had resented her parents for putting their work ahead of her, but gradually she became resigned to their lack of interest and as soon as she was old enough, she left home, leaving them to their insular lives, occasionally wondering if they even noticed she was no longer there.

There was nothing insular about the McGinnis family. No one seemed surprised to find a complete stranger in their midst while they waited for the newest addition to the crowded family tree. She was treated like everyone else. At one point a sleepy baby was plopped down on her lap while the mother went to the restroom. Another time she helped Megan pass around paper cups of coffee for the adults and juice for the children. When a toddler informed her she had to 'go potty,' Clare took her hand and led her to the ladies' restroom, unaware that Kelly's eyes followed her.

About an hour after they had arrived, a nurse dressed in a green scrub uniform came and took the father-to-be away with her. A small boy started to toddle after his father but was whisked up by Kelly and deposited on his grandmother's lap.

The little guy soon fell asleep and Kelly's mother handed him over to one of her daughters-in-law. Kelly's mother picked up the knitting she had temporarily abandoned to comfort her grandson and calmly continued knitting what looked to Clare to be a baby sweater.

Later, Kelly came over to where Clare was playing a game of gin rummy with two of his nieces, using a chair as a playing surface. One of his nieces looked up and greeted her uncle. "Hi, Uncle Kelly. This is Clare."

Smiling while ruffling his niece's coal-black hair, Kelly drawled, "I know, Maire. I brought her here." Turning his attention to Clare, he asked, "Are you all right? Can I get you a sandwich or something? This is taking longer than I expected."

Clare took the card she had just drawn from the pile and laid it down on the discard pile. "I'm fine. The girls have been sharing their candy with me. Maire, you can't draw a card when you've already picked one up off the pile."

Unrepentant, Marie put the card back and grinned up at Kelly. "She's just mad 'cause we've won every game so far. You should teach her how to play, Uncle Kelly. We never beat you."

"That's because I cheat too." Kelly's hand reached out to touch Clare's shoulder, his fingers sliding gently over her delicate bones in sympathy. "Take it easy on her, you guys."

Maire's sister picked up a card off the deck. After rearranging her hand, she splayed out her cards and announced triumphantly, "Gin!"

Clare groaned and gathered the cards from the triumphant winner who stated, "It's your deal, Clare."

Someone called out Kelly's name in the background but before he left her, he asked softly, "If you would rather leave, I can call a taxi to take you home."

Shuffling the cards, Clare shook her head. "I'm just getting the hang of this game. My pride's at stake here. I do have a favor to ask though."

"Anything," he promised, meaning it. "What's the favor?"

She looked up at him and in a sober voice, asked, "If I die of chocolate overdose, will you take care of Sadie?"

Kelly's laughter was a sound of pure delight. "You got it." Bending down, he brushed a light kiss over her mouth and mussed her hair slightly in the same gesture of affection he had bestowed on his niece. Then he was gone.

Clare stared after him, her mouth tingling from the brief contact with his. The deck of cards remained idle in her hands until Maire brought her attention back to the game. "Come on, Clare. Deal the cards. Mommy will be taking us home soon and you need all the practice you can get."

Still dazed by her reaction to Kelly's casual kiss, she began to deal out the cards. Neither of the girls appeared to think the kiss was anything out of the ordinary so she followed their lead. From what she had seen tonight, the whole McGinnis family dispensed kisses and hugs as naturally as breathing.

Always honest with herself, Clare had to admit she would like the kiss to be more than a casual gesture. It certainly hadn't felt casual to her!

"Clare, you're dealing too many cards."

"Sorry." She took back the extra cards and then picked up her hand. She had better pay attention to the game. Right now she had to contend with two adolescent cardsharps.

Later she would worry about dealing with her growing feelings for their uncle.

Three

Exactly at nine in the evening, Patrick Thomas Fitzhugh McGinnis became a new leaf in the McGinnis family tree. The signs of an Irish temper were evident in his lusty crying protests to the world he now found himself in.

Shortly after the proud father announced the arrival of his son, the family crowded around the glass-enclosed nursery for their first glimpse of the latest McGinnis. Clare hung back, not wanting to intrude, but Kelly came for her and stood beside her as they viewed the red-faced infant exercising his little lungs to full capacity. It was the first time Clare had ever seen a newborn baby and she stood in awe of the tiny, squirming, squalling bundle of humanity.

Gradually parents began to gather up their sleepy children to take them home now that the baby had made his grand entrance. Later the hospital would allow the grandparents to hold the new infant, so Kelly's parents were planning to stick around a little longer.

Megan rode down in the elevator with Kelly and

Clare, a faintly wistful expression on her face which made Clare wonder if Megan wished for a baby of her own.

Predictably, the conversation centered around the main character in the evening's proceedings. Megan expressed her opinion about who she thought the baby resembled. "He has Monica's tiny ears and Devlin's nose but he definitely has your mouth, Kel."

Leaning against the back wall of the elevator, Kelly gave his sister a tolerant smile. "How in the world could you tell that? He's so tiny."

Without thinking, Clare contributed, "Probably because his mouth was open most of the time."

Megan burst out laughing while Kelly sent a pained smile in Clare's direction. "Cute."

As they walked out of the hospital, Megan reminded Clare she would be coming to the salon on Tuesday. "I have an appointment with Dorothea for flaws and claws."

Kelly looked completely nonplussed. "What in tarnation is that?"

"I'm getting a facial and my nails done." Heading toward her car which was parked in the opposite direction from Kelly's, she waved good-bye and said over her shoulder, "See you guys later."

Once they were settled in the Blazer, Kelly didn't start the engine right away. Instead he shifted sideways behind the wheel, his arm resting on the back of the seat. "This isn't how I planned to spend the evening with you. I hope you weren't bored."

He had to be kidding, thought Clare with amusement. How could anyone be bored in the midst of a three-ring circus? "I can honestly say I wasn't bored. Frustrated, maybe, but not bored. I never did win a single game of gin rummy. Maire told me she was eight years old but I think she's actually at least thirty. Some of the things she said concerning the birth process were rather startling, but very informative."

Kelly chuckled as he turned the key in the ignition. "She's been a real know-it-all ever since she spent a couple of weeks on my brother's farm. She learned just enough about the facts of life to be a real pain." He backed out of the parking space and drove out of the hospital parking lot. "Did she fill you in on all the details of how her Aunt Monica got pregnant?"

"It was very illuminating," she murmured with amusement. "Not quite accurate but definitely colorful."

They were passing an intersection that Clare recognized. Kelly had either forgotten the way to Mrs. Hamilton's house or he wasn't planning on taking her home right away. "Where are we going?"

"I still owe you dinner. Since most of the restaurants have stopped serving by now, I thought we would go to my place. My refrigerator is better stocked than yours."

She surprised both of them by agreeing with his suggestion without any argument. "Anything but candy."

Clare may have thought she had reached her saturation point for surprises but she was wrong. His 'place' turned out to be an ultra-modern condominium built on the shore of a small man-made lake. The night air had turned chilly and the breeze off the lake was cool as Clare walked beside Kelly under the canopied entrance. Once inside, Kelly closed the door behind them, shutting out the night air. She accompanied him toward the elevator, their footsteps echoing on the tiled floor of the large lobby.

When Kelly unlocked his door and turned on the

light, Clare stared. His home wasn't at all what she expected of Kelly. If he had been a doctor, it would have been appropriate. His apartment was as sterile as an operating room. She had expected his home to reflect some of the work he specialized in but it didn't. It was so colorless, so cold. White walls, glass-and-chrome end tables, gray carpet, gray upholstery covering the contemporary furniture. The only wood she saw was a few split logs stacked on one end of the white brick hearth at the base of the fireplace.

She knew she was staring but she couldn't conceal her surprise. The man was a craftsman in wood, for Pete's sake, and lived in a glass house. It was like a nutritionist who only ate junk food.

When she asked, Kelly showed her where the bathroom was. While she brushed the tangles out of her hair and washed her hands, she glanced around his bathroom which was more chrome, glass, and mirrors. It was ridiculous to feel so disappointed to discover he was living in such a cold environment but she was. His home didn't fit the picture she was beginning to form in her mind about Kelly McGinnis, the man who was warm and caring with his family and took pride in creating beauty in other people's homes. This symphony of glass and chrome wasn't a home where you could relax and put your feet up on the table or munch popcorn on the couch while watching television.

The kitchen was more of the same when she went to find Kelly. There was every modern convenience necessary, with some appliances Clare couldn't even identify. When she entered the kitchen, Kelly was standing in front of a stainless-steel refrigerator removing items and setting them down on the counter.

"What can I do to help?" she offered.

Gesturing toward a cutting board at one end of

the counter, he suggested, "You can be in charge of the salad. You should be able to find everything you need in the refrigerator. I'm in charge of the steaks."

A little later while chopping some tomatoes, Clare asked, "I'm curious about something, Kelly."

Kelly was so surprised she had actually used his name, he almost dropped the knife he had in his hand. He was shocked at the extraordinary pleasure he felt just because she had finally, naturally, used his name. Feeling ridiculous that such a small thing meant so much to him, it took a minute for him to ask, "What are you curious about?"

"Do you remember earlier in my office I mentioned how my customers expect me to use the products I demonstrate and sell?"

"I remember. So?"

"So I'm curious why you live in a contemporary condominium when you specialize in woodworking. I would have thought you would have a house chock-full of custom moldings, pine flooring, carved cornices, that sort of thing."

He didn't reply right away. Clare turned to look at him, feeling a strange tension emanating from him. It wasn't until he put the steaks under the grill in the oven that he turned and met her puzzled gaze.

Leaning a hip against the counter, he crossed his arms over his chest and spoke in a flat tone. "Seven years ago I bought an old abandoned house that looked like it would fall down around my ears if I shut the door too hard. The basic structure was sound but almost everything else had to be torn out and reconstructed. I worked on it whenever I had any spare time and my brothers took pity on me and helped when they could. After about a year of working on it, I was able to move into one of the rooms and start on the interior, putting in all the custom work I had learned over the years, installing hand-carved door panels, fluting and shell carvings on the fireplaces, door frames, and decorative moldings. I had pilastered windows, hand-carved banisters, a custom-canopied bed."

Suddenly he ended his description of the house, the faraway look in his eyes changing, a haunted, painful expression creating shadows where a glow of pride had been.

"It sounds wonderful." Hating to ask but needing to know, Clare asked softly, "What happened to the house?"

In a resigned tone edged with bitterness, Kelly stated bluntly, "A demolition team flattened it one day."

Clare's eyes widened in shock. Her voice was a mere whisper as she asked, "Why?"

"My ex-wife's divorce lawyer was better than mine. She ended up with the house, which she promptly sold to a developer who tore it down and shoved up a bunch of condominiums." He then added quietly, "On Cunningham Street."

Clare gaped in horror. No wonder he had been so angry out at Mrs. Hamilton's when she had told him about the garden plots used by the residents of the condominiums on Cunningham Street. The people who planted carrots and cucumbers on Mrs. Hamilton's property lived where his house had been.

Sometimes life could take some bizarre twists but this time fate had outdone itself.

Feeling incredibly sad, she murmured inadequately, "I'm sorry."

"Why should you feel sorry? It wasn't your fault." With cool steadiness, he answered her earlier reference to his current living quarters. "I put too much of myself into that other house only to have it destroyed by a demolition crew. I don't have anything left to put into another one of my own so I bought this antiseptic cell."

He turned the steaks over and Clare went back to preparing the salad, her thoughts full of what he had told her. The cruel disposal of his other house explained why he had reacted so strongly to the sight of the garden plots and greenhouses spoiling the beauty of the grounds around Mrs. Hamilton's beautiful old home. It must have seemed like an abomination to him. His resentment toward losing his own house could have carried over since she was doing what his ex-wife had done, selling off a treasure from the past, a home where love and care had been grooved into every board. She didn't plan to destroy the house, but she was going to have to sell it. And while her reasons may have been different, money was the motivating factor as had been the case with his ex-wife.

Clare discovered she was curious about Kelly's ex-wife. Was she beautiful? What had gone wrong with their marriage? Did Kelly still harbor feelings other than resentment and bitterness toward her? Since they were questions she would not ask, she would never know the answers.

Kelly's house wasn't mentioned again. Strangely enough, Clare didn't feel the time was right to bring up the subject of the estimates on Mrs. Hamilton's house so soon after Kelly had told her about losing his own.

The steaks were done to perfection and they sat down to the late meal at a glass table in the dining room. They were both ravenous and concentrated on their meal. Over coffee, Kelly related some unusual and often humorous incidents which had taken place during his time in Colonial Williamsburg. She, in turn, told him about some of her less-than-successful experiences while studying for her cosmetology degree.

After dinner while Kelly was wiping the dishes Clare washed, she commented, "You have a remarkable family, but then I imagine you already know that."

Suddenly there was an odd, guarded expression in his eyes. He replied, "I'm not sure what you mean by remarkable."

Good grief, she thought wearily. Had she wandered over into another touchy subject? Maybe she should stick to the weather. "I meant your family seems to be very close to each other. If something happens to one, it affects everyone. Like tonight at the hospital, for instance."

"Last night. It happens to be almost two o'clock in the morning."

"All right. Last night. Your family was on hand to give support to the parents and to welcome the newest little McGinnis. Maire told me about the time one of her uncles, the one with the farm, had an accident with a piece of machinery. After she finished a disgustingly graphic description of the injury, she went on to tell how the rest of the family immediately came out to take over the chores until your brother could do them himself. It must be wonderful to be able to count on your family like that."

His eyes were curious although his question was casual. "Don't you have any family?"

"I'm an only child. My parents are successful lawyers in Maryland. Very ambitious, very motivated. My mother occasionally remembers to acknowledge my birthday with a card and I get a token package every Christmas but that's the extent of the Denham family feeling. I suppose that's why I am so impressed with yours."

Kelly examined her face thoroughly, wishing he knew whether or not she was telling the truth or simply giving him what she thought he wanted to hear. His ex-wife had been enthusiastic about his family too at one time until they were married. Then she began to resent the closeness and possessiveness of his family.

Well, it didn't really matter what Clare's opinion was, he decided. She was only going to be in his life for a short time anyway, long enough to warm his bed until he tired of her like the other women he had been involved with briefly. Maybe if he told himself over and over that she was just another woman, he might even believe it.

Folding the towel she had used to dry her hands, she said, "I envy you."

Startled by her statement, he asked, "Why?"

"Your family is very affectionate toward each other, very open and natural. My parents didn't encourage signs of affection. I find it fascinating to see how you and your family move in tandem, depending on each other, loving each other." With a self-conscious laugh, she added, "Boy, I must be more tired than I thought. I didn't mean to say all that."

She might hate herself later for opening up to him, but Kelly was glad she had. It explained a lot about her.

He reached out and took the towel from her and placed it on the counter before touching her face gently.

"It's late. I'd better get you home."

Clare hated to have the unusual evening and morning end, but he was right. It was time for her to go home. She suddenly felt extremely tired, worn out by the myriad of sights, scenes, and emotions she had experienced.

The trip back to her house was uneventful. There

were no police sirens this time, only soft music from the radio. Kelly left the Blazer's lights on to illuminate their way to Clare's front door since she hadn't turned the outside lamps on before she had left.

At the door, he took her house key and unlocked the door, reaching in to flick on the inside hall light before handing back her keys.

All of a sudden, Clare exclaimed, "I don't believe it!"

Startled, Kelly asked, "Don't believe what?"

"We never got around to discussing the estimate on the work that needs to be done on this house."

He didn't seem too concerned about it. "I'm too exhausted to talk figures now. I'll give you a call tomorrow and we can set up another time to go over the estimates." All of a sudden he grinned down at her. "None of my other sisters-in-law are pregnant that I know of so we shouldn't be interrupted."

Yawning widely, Clare covered her mouth with her hand and mumbled, "All right. I guess one more day won't matter."

Kelly gazed down at her and thought how sweet she looked with her hair tousled by the wind and exhaustion shadowing her eyes, giving them a dreamy expression. "The estimates will give me an excuse to see you again."

Her sleepy eyes widened in surprise but she didn't say anything. She couldn't. It was suddenly all she could do to breathe.

Without realizing he was going to touch her, Kelly's hands reached for her and brought her into his warm body, his head lowering to find her mouth.

The kiss was flame and smoke, searing his blood and clouding his judgment. He had only meant to kiss her good night, but the minute he felt her soft alluring lips under his, he remembered how unsatisfactory the brief kiss had been at the hospital and how he had wanted to taste more of her. Now he could.

When the pressure of his lips broke open her mouth, Clare sighed softly, her warm breath flowing into his mouth as he deepened the kiss. His arms tightened around her and her back arched to press her yearning softness against the heat and strength of his strong body. Her exhaustion was replaced with other feelings, an aching need, a throbbing awareness of his thudding heartbeat against her breasts.

Kelly ground his mouth into hers, his tongue delving into the intimate softness of her mouth, tasting and savoring the sweetness of her. His hands moved over her back and her hips, molding her to him like a pliant clay form created to conform to his shape. But this was no piece of clay he held in his arms. This was a warm, exciting, intoxicating, intriguing woman who was driving his control to a dangerous level with those soft kitten sounds she made when his mouth forged forcefully against hers.

Clare wanted to touch him as he was touching her but when she raised her hands to his chest, he brought his hands up to hers and pried them down, his fingers lacing through hers, keeping their clasped hands pressed against his thighs. She made a sound of frustration but he didn't give in to it. If he was to maintain any semblance of control at all, he would have to keep her hands off his body.

He contented himself with exploring her mouth, moving his lips over hers and running his tongue over her lips, teasing and exploring—until she wanted more. Her teeth nipped his bottom lip and he felt a surge of need so strong, he took her mouth almost savagely, driving them both near the edge—but he still kept her hands clasped.

A fierce satisfaction like nothing he had ever felt

before coiled through him. He was not alone in this. She wanted him too.

Suddenly he froze as if a torrent of ice water had been thrown over him. This wasn't a woman he could calmly take and walk away from. This was the kind of woman he stayed away from. He had to run now before he was caught in the spell she was weaving around him.

He tore his hands from hers and slowly began to back away from her. Staring at him, Clare could see the look of near horror on his face and the negative shake of his head. She heard his low mumbled repetition of one word. *No.* He kept repeating it like a chant to ward off whatever demons he had conjured up.

"Kelly?" she asked hesitantly. "What's wrong?"

He was almost to the steps, and he stared at her long and hard before replying, "You." As though saying it again made it true, he repeated, "You, Clare. You. This. Us."

Turning away abruptly, he walked swiftly to the Blazer and the tires spun gravel as he sped away.

Stunned, Clare couldn't move, her eyes following the receding red lights until they were out of sight. Her body began to shake with reaction and her hand came up to rub her mouth as if she could forcibly remove the imprint of his lips. Then she slowly entered the empty house.

Leaving only the hall light on, she went into the living room and sank down onto the sofa, staring into the dark space. What had gone wrong? He had kissed her thoroughly, exacting pleasure in every touch, every kiss. She could have sworn he had been as involved as she had been. He had kissed her with a hunger to match hers and then suddenly had acted as though they had just committed some unspeakable act.

What had he meant when he had said she was all wrong? They were all wrong? Wrong for what? For kissing? How could anything that felt so good be wrong?

Anger and disappointment replaced the hurt and humiliation. She might not be the answer to every man's wildest dreams but damn it, she certainly didn't deserve to be treated as though she were diseased.

She would find someone else to do the repairs on the house. Some kindly old man with a dozen grandchildren. A lovely old goat who wouldn't give her any guff about the whys and wherefores of what she wanted done. She would definitely make sure that whoever she hired didn't have black hair, blue eyes, or a drop of Irish blood in him.

Four

For the rest of the weekend Clare did her darndest to blot Kelly from her mind. Trying to figure out why he had acted so strange was like flogging a dead horse. It didn't accomplish a thing.

However, against her will, images flickered through her mind like an old silent film, images of the glint of amusement in his eyes, his rich laugh, his lithe grace—and the horrified expression on his face when he had backed away from her. No matter how many times the scene played over in her mind, she couldn't come up with a valid reason for his peculiar behavior. Her instincts, her female intuition couldn't have been so wrong. He had been as involved as she was in the wild pleasure they had given each other. His aroused hard body had been pressed against hers and his hands had held hers as though he never wanted to let her go.

Every time she thought about him, she became angry, but dwelling on what might have been was a luxury she couldn't afford. But then, she reminded herself grimly, there was a lot she couldn't afford right now. There was a stack of bills on the antique desk in Mrs. Hamilton's house to prove that fact.

Determined to carry on as usual after the disastrous exit of Kelly McGinnis from her life, she spent Sunday cleaning Mrs. Hamilton's house. Even though the house was legally in her name, Clare always thought of it as Mrs. Hamilton's. To her, it was an obligation, a responsibility, and that's all she wanted it to be. The house held years of memories for Mrs. Hamilton and her ancestors but there were none for Clare, and she didn't want any. She would clean it, repair it, and try to sell it, but she didn't want to become fond of the old place. Becoming attached to Mrs. Hamilton's house would cause too many heartaches when it was sold—and it had to be sold.

Her feelings of obligation toward Mrs. Hamilton weren't based entirely on gratitude. The older woman had given her a job when she desperately needed one, she had loaned her the money for tuition in order to get her degree, and she had been supportive and caring throughout their acquaintance. Clare was grateful, but she stayed mostly because the older woman needed her now that she was so ill, not only financially but as a friend. No one else had ever needed her and she liked the feeling.

What she didn't need was the complication of a man who acted as if she was Venus one minute and Quasimodo the next.

By Tuesday she had finally managed to put the whole episode of Kelly McGinnis behind her, at least most of the time. The salon was busier than ever. Along with the usual multitude of clients, the mall was undergoing decoration for a spring promotion. She had to decorate her display window to blend in with the mall's theme. This on top of her usual schedule of appointments and endless paperwork left her with little spare time for idle musings.

She had forgotten about Megan's appointment until she saw Kelly's sister enter the salon. It was too much to hope Megan would keep off the subject of her brother. She didn't.

In fact Megan mentioned him as soon as she sat down next to the work station where Clare was applying makeup to a regular customer. After greeting Clare and several other women, she adjusted the protective covering Dorothea draped around her neck and stated, "I talked to Kelly on the phone yesterday. He sounded as happy as a bear with a thorn in his paw. When I asked him if he was going to do the repairs for you, he snarled at me and told me to mind my own business."

Clare could feel the inquisitive antennae rise among the other women. In an attempt to deflect their interest, she stated, "It sounds like good advice to me."

"Maybe it's good advice but it's not much fun. I'll ask you instead of Kelly. Is Kelly going to do the repairs for you?"

"I don't think so."

"Why not?"

Clare had to admire Megan's perseverance. She wasn't about to tell Megan that she and Kelly had never gotten around to discussing the repairs. If she did, Megan would undoubtedly be persistent enough to ask what they had been discussing instead.

"I'm having second thoughts about having the work done at all."

Her customer jumped in to tell her she was wise to be wary about having work done on her house, and proceeded to tell her about an experience she'd had when carpenters tore out her old cabinets to replace them with new ones. She listed various complaints about workmen not showing up on schedule, sawdust throughout the house, and the continual noise of electric saws and pounding hammers.

Clare made the appropriate sympathetic remarks, relieved to have the subject changed. Several other women had their own horror stories to tell, and Clare encouraged them. Anything to keep Megan from resuming her duties as matchmaker. The last person she wanted to discuss was Kelly McGinnis. The last person she wanted to think about was Kelly McGinnis.

She was filling out an order for stock for the salon late in the afternoon when the receptionist put a call through. Expecting to hear one of her clients, she was startled when Kelly's deep voice came over the wire.

"Clare, it's Kelly."

After a brief pause, Clare asked, "Yes?"

Kelly half-expected frost to coat the receiver. "Clare, I need to talk to you."

"I'm busy, Mr. McGinnis. If you want a facial, make an appointment. Otherwise we have nothing to discuss." Then she hung up. Buzzing the receptionist quickly, she instructed her to hold all calls from Mr. Kelly McGinnis. Whatever he wanted, she didn't want to hear it. At least that's what she kept telling herself.

When Clare was leaving at six o'clock, the receptionist handed her a stack of messages. All but two were from Kelly with instructions to phone him at the different numbers he had left. Those she wadded up and threw in the receptionist's wastebasket.

That evening she sat at the kitchen table with the evening paper turned to the classified section and the yellow pages of the telephone book open to the pages listing carpenters. In between sipping a cup of coffee and munching on a sandwich, she made a list of carpenters to phone in the morning, noting as she ran through the lists that only one of them advertised himself as a craftsman. Kelly McGinnis, woodwright. His name was not added to her list.

When she arrived at the salon the following morning, she made phone calls to the names on her list. After thirty minutes, she had crossed off every one. They didn't give free estimates, or they didn't want to tackle the problems associated with working on an old house, or else they couldn't promise to come out until sometime in 1990.

Throwing her pen onto her desk in frustration, she slumped back in her chair and scowled at the phone as though it was all the phone's fault. She went over the options. If the repairs didn't get done, she was going to have to lower the selling price for the house. That would be a more practical solution than paying someone to do the repairs out of her own pocket. But she preferred to have the house in mint condition before turning it over to the new owner. The house deserved to look its best.

The red light blinked on her phone intercom indicating the receptionist was announcing her next appointment. But it wasn't her next appointment.

Denise sounded unusually hesitant. "Mr. McGinnis is on line two, Miss Denham. I know you told me to take a message if he phoned again but he insists he has to talk to you."

"Tell Mr. McGinnis to go float on a rock."

"Excuse me?"

"Never mind, Denise," she sighed wearily. "I'll take the call."

She punched the button for line two and snapped rudely, "What do you want, McGinnis?"

"I want to talk to you."

"You are talking to me."

He tried again. "I want to see you. I need to explain about the other night but not over the phone.

I'll meet you anytime, anyplace you say but I have to talk to you."

Clare steeled herself against the warm persuasive voice. "There's no need to explain anything. You made yourself perfectly clear. Now it's my turn to make things clear. Don't call me again."

As she was hanging up the phone, she could hear his voice raised as he called her name, but she cut him off.

A few minutes later, the red light came back on but it wasn't Kelly. The receptionist announced her next appointment had arrived.

Later, when she was getting ready to leave for the day, one of the beauty consultants asked her if she could take a late lunch the following day.

"As long as you make sure you don't have an appointment during the time you want off, I don't mind."

Stella confirmed. "I've checked the appointment book. I'm clear from two to three. I'll be back in plenty of time for my three o'clock. All I wanted to do was run to the hardware store to pick up some parts I ordered for my kitchen faucet."

Knowing Stella was divorced with two young children, Clare asked, "You're going to fix your own plumbing?"

"Sure. Repairmen cost too much. I try to fix what I can myself."

"How do you know what to do?"

Stella dug through the variety of things she carried in the large canvas bag slung over her shoulder and drew out a thin, oversized book. "I buy a how-to book. This one is on plumbing repairs."

Leafing through the book, Clare saw step-by-step instructions accompanied with clear drawings and comprehensive photographs. A sudden idea made Clare ask, "Are there instruction books for other types of repairs?"

Stella nodded. "Electrical, plumbing, ceramic tile, woodworking. You name it, there's a manual for it."

A few minutes later, Clare had the name and address of the hardware store where Stella told her she could find the equipment and instruction manuals she needed.

That evening, Kelly drove up the long lane leading to Clare's house. Phoning her was accomplishing nothing except to stoke his Irish temper. It had been stoked to the boiling point each time she had hung up on him, and it was still simmering. Whether Miss Denham liked it or not, she no longer had a choice about where or when they were going to talk. She was going to see him tonight. If she wasn't home, he would wait.

There were no lights on in the house, at least none that he could see from the front. She could be in either the kitchen or her bedroom, both rooms located at the back of the house. He parked in front and got out of his car. He had driven his BMW instead of the Blazer since she would recognize his truck. He was using any advantage he could think of to make sure she didn't refuse to open the door.

Heading toward the front door, he stopped halfway up the steps when he heard a familiar sound coming from the side of the house. Then heard it again. What in hell? he asked himself. He recognized the whining noise as one he heard every day. It was a power saw. If she had hired somebody else to do the repairs on the house, he was going to wring her neck.

Hurrying around the corner of the house, he saw a light shining from the window in the garage. Approaching the building, he heard another familiar sound. Someone was hammering. The side door was ajar and he headed for it, pushing the wooden door open just enough to see into the garage. For a moment, he could only stare, unable to believe what he was seeing.

Clare was standing in front of an old wooden workbench that had been built along one wall of the large two-car garage. She was wearing a pair of faded jeans, a denim shirt over what looked like a man's white T-shirt, a red bandana rolled and tied around her forehead, and her hair tied into a low ponytail at the nape of her neck. Even though she had sawdust in her hair, wore no makeup, and was dressed like a slender stevedore, he had never seen her look more desirable.

She held a hammer in her right hand, while her left hand held down a page of a book propped up in front of her. Then he saw her pick up a small board and place it on top of another one on the bench in front of her. She took a long nail out of a sack, positioned it on the board, and lifted the hammer.

That's when Kelly shoved the door open wider and shouted, "What in hell are you doing?"

Instead of hitting the nail, the hammer landed smack dab on her thumb. Crying out, she dropped the hammer onto the workbench and grabbed her throbbing thumb.

Moving quickly, Kelly edged around in front of her car parked in one half of the garage, nearly tripping over several clay flowerpots in his haste to get to her. Finally reaching her, his hand closed around her wrist so he could examine her battered thumb. The blow had missed her fingernail but the thumb was red and beginning to swell. Having banged his own fingers a time or two the same way, he knew how it felt and what type of first aid to administer.

His fury needed some sort of outlet and she was handy. "Look what you've done, you little idiot."

"It's your fault," she retaliated angrily. "If you hadn't startled me, I would have hit the nail and not my thumb."

"You shouldn't have been using a hammer in the first place," Starting toward the door, he hauled her after him. "Come on. We need to put some ice on that thumb."

Tugging at the wrist he held captive, she protested, "*We* don't have to do anything, Mr. McGinnis. This happens to be *my* thumb, thank you very much. Besides you're trespassing."

He was in no mood to debate property rights. He was downright furious. Furious because she had hurt herself, furious because he hadn't been able to stop it, and furious because she had put herself in a situation where she could be hurt.

Still resisting the strong grip on her wrist and his proprietorial attitude, she stated heatedly, "I have work to do so you just go out the way you came in and let me get back to what I was doing."

"Are you going to try for the other nine fingers?" he asked nastily. "Leave whatever it is you're trying to do while you still have your remaining fingers. Unless you plan to go to the salon tomorrow with a thumb that looks like a foot, you'd better let me put some ice on it now."

Clare knew he was right but she hated to admit it. Her darn thumb was hurting like the dickens and she knew she was going to have to do as he said. But she didn't have to like it.

"First I have to unplug the saw."

He stared down at her in disbelief. "What?"

"The instructions that came with the saw stated it should be unplugged when not in use," she explained reasonably, adding disdainfully, "You of all people should know that, Mr. Woodwright. Oh, but I forgot. You don't use modern power tools, do you? Those noisy contraptions don't fit into your image as a craftsman. Take my word for it. The saw is supposed to be unplugged."

"I do live in this century," he snapped back.

Keeping his fingers firmly around her wrist, he looked around and saw that the power saw was on the bench: a nice, new, shiny saber saw. A small pile of sawdust lay next to a freshly sawed board. Then he noticed the book. Reaching out with his free hand, he flipped the book closed so he could read the cover. In bold print, he read the words, *Woodworking Made Easy.*

Bringing his gaze back to her, his eyes were blue chips of ice, his anger a tangible force in the close confines of the dusty garage. He muttered several picturesque Gaelic curses when it dawned on him the screwy woman was planning to try to do the repairs on the house herself. He didn't trust himself to say anything else. He jerked the plug of the saw from the socket before turning back toward the side door of the garage, bringing her with him.

"I'm not going anywhere with you," she protested as she was forced to stumble after him, unable to break the hold he had on her wrist. "I'm not through in here yet."

"Like hell you aren't." The palm of his free hand slapped the surface of the side door and flung it open. Because of his tour of the house last week, Kelly knew where the side entrance to the house was and drew her toward it. Luckily it was unlocked. He pulled her up the three steps leading from a utility room into the kitchen. Even in his fury, he was careful of her injured thumb as he maneuvered her around the counters and settled her into a chair at the table.

"Stay put," he ordered, his tone daring her to disobey him.

As though the kitchen were his instead of hers, he unerringly found everything he needed. In a few minutes, he had crushed ice cubes in a plastic bag which he placed on her thumb after taking her hand and positioning it palm up on the table top, ignoring the glowering look she gave him. Using his own handkerchief, he had folded it several times before laying it over her thumb before he had applied the improvised ice bag.

"Leave the ice there for awhile. It will keep the swelling down."

"All right," she murmured grudgingly. She watched as he pulled out the chair opposite her and sat down. "Now that you've done your bit as Dr. Welby, will you tell me why you're here? The other night you couldn't wait to get away from me."

"The other night is what I wanted to talk to you about when I called you." His voice hardened. "But you kept cutting me off."

The ice bag slipped off and she sat it back in place. "Is business that bad?"

Unable to fathom what she meant, he stared at her blankly. "What are you talking about?"

"I work with the public too, remember? It's not necessary to like your clients in order to work for them."

His anger faded away, to be replaced by confusion. "You've lost me. You'll have to spell that out for me, Lily."

"If you're here about the estimates on the house, you don't need to bother apologizing for the other night. For one thing, it isn't necessary to kiss clients in order to take on their work and secondly, I decided to do the repairs myself."

Kelly stared at her long and hard. It was odd how perfectly normal some crazy people could look. She had everything more tangled up than the ball of knitting yarn his grandmother's dog had got hold of one afternoon. He continued to study her. Each time he had been with her, he had seen a different woman and it wasn't only her appearance. She had as many variations as a complicated symphony. There was nothing obvious about Clare Denham. She defied description. She also defied understanding.

"Clare," he said patiently. "What happened between us the other night has nothing to do with whether I do the repairs on this house. One is personal, the other is business."

"Which one explains why you're here?"

His jaw clamped tightly in irritation at the coolness in her voice. He was accustomed to fiery debates with the women in his family. If his sisters weren't happy about something, he and half the world knew about it. A little healthy temper from Clare would have been helpful. Anything but her calm expression and cool attitude which gave him the impression she didn't give a tinker's hoot what he did or thought.

His mother and sisters were easy to read, like an open book with large print. Clare, on the other hand, was as easy to read as hieroglyphics on an ancient tomb.

Maybe a bit of plain speaking would get some sort of honest reaction from her. Leaning his arms on the table, he looked directly into her eyes. "I wanted you the other night, Clare. I wanted you very badly. When I started to kiss you, I had only one objective and that was to get you into bed." He paused to let his words soak in. "But then I changed my mind."

"I noticed." In case he could see the hurt she was afraid she wasn't able to conceal, she let the ice bag fall onto the table and got up. Going to the refrigerator, she asked politely, "Would you like some iced tea?"

Kelly's chair scraped against the wooden floor as he pushed back his chair. "Will you sit down, for crying out loud? You would try the patience of St. Patrick himself. That ice isn't going to do any good melting away on the table."

She looked down at his hand holding her wrist. He seemed to be doing that a lot lately, she thought inconsequently. The expression in his eyes made her think he would prefer to have his fingers closed around her throat. Whew! He sure got mad easily.

The pressure of his fingers tightened and she returned to her chair. He replaced the ice bag on her thumb before he went to the refrigerator. In a few minutes, he put two glasses of iced tea on the table. He didn't ask if she wanted any sugar, and she didn't make an issue out of the fact that she liked a little sweetener in her iced tea. There was a time for asserting oneself over important issues and another time for keeping one's trap shut when the issue was minor.

Sitting down across from her, Kelly leaned back in his chair, his eyes glinting like chips of blue glass as he gazed at her. "We're going to talk about the other night, Clare. I'm not leaving until we do."

"Why is it so important to talk about it? I would just as soon forget about it."

"My Gran used to say it's easy to prove someone's a fool if they continually act like one. I acted like a first-class fool when I left you so abruptly without any explanation. The last couple of days I've thought about nothing else but you and what you must be thinking. You deserve to know why I turned away from you. I don't want you to think it has anything to do with anything you might have done."

Clare simply waited. Her pride wanted to hear his explanation but that same pride kept her from demanding it.

Coming forward in his chair, Kelly again leaned his arms on the table, Brutally frank, he began, "After I brought you home from my place, I had every intention of getting myself invited into your house and then your bedroom. After you responded to me like you did when I kissed you, I didn't expect any resistance." He read her expression correctly, and his mouth curved in a rueful smile. "I know. I know. I'm an arrogant bastard. You can't think up any names I haven't already called myself."

"I could debate that but I won't. Go on."

"At first it was all so simple. I wanted you; therefore I was going to take you and get rid of the need to make love to you. It was all very basic, very logical. Then suddenly everything got very complicated."

Clare was so intent on what he was saying, she didn't notice the ice bag was slowly slipping off her hand again. Kelly reached over and adjusted the bag but didn't withdraw his hand once the bag was back in place. His fingers toyed with hers, needing the contact, his eyes resting on the delicate bones of her hand.

His voice became low, a hint of seriousness in his eyes. "I might have been able to go through with my original plans if somewhere along the line I hadn't realized I wanted more than one night with you. Suddenly you were more than a body to satisfy the lust in mine. I couldn't use you like that. When I realized that, I had to leave. I never considered myself a coward before but I certainly turned into one that night. I virtually ran for my life!"

Clare hadn't expected such honesty from him. Now she understood why he had said she was all wrong. He had meant she was all wrong for a one-night stand. But she still didn't understand why he felt compelled to make such a point of confessing the reasons for his actions. "Why tell me all this? Why not just mark it down as one of fate's little witticisms? I'm a big brave girl who doesn't expect every man to be Prince Charming. I admit I was confused when one minute you were kissing me as though you were enjoying it and the next minute acting as though you had kissed a toad but I would have survived without an explanation. You may not have remained my favorite person but I wasn't heartbroken, just confused."

His fingers tightened around hers. "Clare, I want to be your favorite man, at least for a while. I still want you, but nothing has changed. I don't want to commit myself to any one woman again. I would like to go on seeing you but not with any promises of a future together. I don't think you're the type of woman to accept a brief affair, but I can't let you go on thinking we would ever have anything more than that. After giving it a lot of thought I decided I would give you your choice of telling me to drive off the nearest cliff or agreeing to my conditions. We don't even have to become intimate but I do want to go on seeing you."

She pulled her hand back. He had given her a lot to think about and she didn't need his touch to confuse her any more than she already was. He said she wasn't the type of woman to have an affair, yet that's what he was offering. Wasn't it? He could spout noble gestures about not becoming intimate, but how long would that last? It would be easier to stop the tide from changing. Even now she could feel the current tugging at her, whirling around in her bloodstream.

Her silence was driving him crazy. He needed an answer, damn it. The last couple of days had been a living hell without her. He needed to know if he could at least go on seeing her even if it meant not being able to give in to the desire she created in him. "Well?" he prodded. "Haven't you heard a thing I said? Don't you have anything to say?"

She needed time to think and he wasn't giving it to her. "I heard you. I may have bashed my thumb but my hearing is just fine." Needing to put some distance between them, she pushed back her chair and grabbed the bag of melting ice, throwing it in the sink with considerable force. Damn his hide, anyway. She was actually considering taking him up on his preposterous suggestion. She really was tempted and that made her mad.

His impatience changed to amusement. So she had a temper after all! She just had a different way of expressing it. He felt as though he needed a crowbar to get her to admit how she felt about his proposition. He decided to use patience instead.

A full five minutes passed. Kelly sipped at his glass of iced tea and Clare stared out the window over the sink.

Finally, Clare turned around and faced him. "When would we start?"

Kelly had been in the process of drinking when she spoke and nearly choked. Gasping for air, he croaked, "Start what?"

"This affair or friendship or buddy system, whatever you want to call it."

Kelly attempted to recover his breath and his senses. If he heard correctly, she had just agreed to have an affair with him. So why did he get the feeling he should be happier than he was? It was what he wanted too. Wasn't it? Somehow this wasn't going the way it was supposed to go.

Having no prior experience with such an unorthodox offer, Clare was mystified by his reaction, or, to be more explicit, his lack of action. She wasn't expecting him to jump up and down with joy but he didn't have to look as if he had just been punched in the stomach.

She came back to the table and sat down. "For reasons of my own, I don't want any serious involvement right now either. But I enjoy being with you and I like the way you make me feel, so I'm going along with your, ah, proposition—with a few conditions. I won't make any demands on you and I won't expect any from you. We each have our work and other commitments which will require our time. If either of us wants to go our separate way, we say so and there will be no hard feelings, no recriminations. We're both adults and should be able to handle this . . . relationship without things getting messy and emotional."

Kelly played back every word she had said in his mind, wondering why they didn't sound right, even though it was what he wanted to hear, what he thought he wanted to hear.

When he didn't say anything, Clare asked, "What do we do now? Shake hands or something?"

"*NO!* Damn it! We don't." His chair nearly tipped over as he shoved it back. He got to his feet and came around the table. His hands gripped her shoulders almost painfully, certainly angrily, and pulled her up to stand in front of him. His mouth was rough as he took hers violently. For a man who was getting what he wanted, there was a desperate quality in the way his arms closed around her, holding her securely as though he wanted to imprint her into his body, as though she would vanish in a wisp of smoke if he didn't hold on to her tightly.

Finally breaking his mouth away from hers, he asked huskily, "Are you sure this is what you want?"

Her arms had gone up around his neck when he had first pulled her into his arms. They now moved to the back of his head to bring his mouth back to hers. Against his lips, she whispered, "Yes. You couldn't have come into my life at a worse time but

I've never wanted a man like this. It's like my insides are falling apart and you're the only person who can put me back together."

Kelly found it hard to breathe as though his heart was being squeezed by a delicate fist. Her declaration was unexpected and hit him hard. The sound of thunder echoed in his ears even though it was a clear evening without a cloud in the sky. Then he realized it was his heart thudding in his chest, his blood roaring in his ears.

As he took the lips she was offering, he wondered why she didn't want to be seriously involved right now and why this was such a bad time for her. But when her tongue stroked his, everything else was obliterated from his mind except the glorious taste of her.

The physical attraction between them was almost too strong to continue like this without becoming lovers. Almost. Neither Kelly nor Clare was ready to cross into that territory at this point, fearing they might not be able to find their way back. It was too new, too fragile.

For now they sealed their agreement with hot, hungry kisses and searching tongues, knowing that the day would come when their need would overcome their individual cautions.

Kelly's control was hanging by a frail thread when he lifted his mouth from the delectable pulse below her ear and loosened his arms enough to look down into her molten gold eyes, amazed at her natural sensuality. He felt more of a man with her than he could ever remember feeling with any other woman. He gloried in it, marveled at it, and like the other night, felt an unreasonable fear because of it.

With his smile a little off center, he set her away from him. "Maybe shaking hands wasn't such a bad idea."

"You aren't going to make a mad dash for your car again, are you?"

Giving her a brief kiss, he brought her back to the table and set her back down. "Not this time, although if I had any sense, I would. Being around you is hard on my blood pressure but great on the eyes, so I'm going to give my blood pressure a rest and take advantage of the chance to look at you." He went back to the freezer. "But first, I'm going to get a fresh ice bag for that thumb and then I'm going to sit down with the solid table between us and listen to you tell me all about your new hobby."

"Which new hobby is that?"

"The one out in the garage. The one that involves saws, hammers, and sawdust, and creates funny-looking thumbs."

Once she told him about her plans to attempt the repairs herself, oddly enough he made no comment. She thought he would try to talk her out of it but he didn't.

In fact he was unusually quiet the rest of the time he was there, which wasn't very long. After finishing his drink, he got up and said he had to leave.

Walking him to the door, Clare accepted his hard kiss and watched him walk to his car, a puzzled frown marring her features.

If this was an affair, it was about as exciting as a basket of eggs.

Five

The following morning, Kelly phoned her at a ridiculously early hour to ask her to meet him for lunch.

Because she was waiting for her heartbeat to return to normal from being startled out of a sound sleep and was yawning so widely her jaw was in danger of dislocating, she wasn't able to answer right away. At least not fast enough to suit Kelly.

"Clare, I can hear you breathing. Answer me."

She managed a sound that was a cross between a moan and a grunt. Glancing at the small clock on her bedside table, she saw the directions the hands were pointing. "Good lord, Kelly. It's six o'clock in the morning!"

"I can tell time, Lily," he replied with slight sarcasm and then switched to what he considered more important.

"How's your thumb?"

"It's all right. A little sore and black and blue but the ice did the trick."

He returned to his first question.

"What about lunch?"

Her mental gears were finally beginning to mesh. She reminded him it was Wednesday, the day he usually had lunch with Megan. He invited her to join them but Clare declined. Wednesday was her day for visiting Mrs. Hamilton, but she didn't mention that to Kelly.

"I have plans that can't be changed, Kelly," she explained, and left it at that.

Kelly bit back all the questions he had regarding her plans for the day. Their relationship was too new and tenuous to start making demands at this point. One of her conditions was that they each had commitments on their time and they had to respect each other's privacy. At the time, he hadn't realized how difficult it was going to be not knowing what those demands on her time were.

It was curious. He had never been particularly interested in what occupied the time of other women he had dated, not even his own wife. What they did when he wasn't with them had never concerned him. It was different with Clare. He wanted to know everything she did, was going to do, who she was going to do it with, why she was going to do it. And he wanted to know it all *now*.

He remembered his Gran had once told him he reminded her of a frog she used to watch in her garden. This frog would leap ahead without looking, usually bumping into one obstacle after another before finally reaching his destination. Kelly had known his Gran had used her unique way of telling a story to make a point. This point was about his impulsive behavior, to look before he leaped.

He had never found it to be so darn difficult to think before he acted as he did with Clare. With her, he wanted it all right now, if not sooner.

Sprawled on his bed, he cradled the receiver in the hollow of his neck, wishing she was there beside him instead of on the other side of a thin filament line courtesy of the phone company. Her husky, just-awakened voice was sending hot messages to his body that would be left unanswered under the circumstances. Here he was naked in his large bed in his condominium, and out in the country, Clare was alone in her antique bed in that old house.

His thoughts forced him to ask, "What are you wearing?"

"I never knew you had an interest in ladies' lingerie, Kelly," she replied with a smile in her voice.

"I'm broadening my horizons. Humor me."

"You don't think it's a little early in the morning to be broadening horizons?"

"Six A.M. is as good a time as any."

A teasing note lightened her sleepy tones. "There isn't much to describe."

His fingers clenched the rumpled sheets of the bed. "Wonderful," he drawled hoarsely. "You might as well continue, Lily. Whatever you have on can't make me any crazier than imagining you wearing nothing at all."

Even if she hadn't been wearing a gift from Madeleine, Clare would have been tempted to make up a provocative description of a seduction nightgown just to see what his reaction would be. But all she had to do was tell him the truth. "It's a short baby-doll that ends up at the top of my thighs. There is lace around the bottom and also several inches of lace down the front. It's a soft peach color and is made of satin with narrow, almost nonexistent straps. There are three tiny pearl buttons down the front that keep coming undone and . . ."

"That's enough," he interrupted. "I get the picture. Just out of curiosity, is this your usual night-time attire?"

"A friend of mine gave it to me for my birthday. She said it would do wonders for my morale."

"I can't say it's doing much for mine."

"You asked."

"So I did. It wouldn't be the first time my mouth overcame my good sense. Now would be a perfect time to change the subject, like asking you when I can see you again since lunch has been ruled out. How about dinner tonight?"

"Well," she began hesitantly. "I had sort of made some plans. There's an outdoor concert in the park and I was looking forward to a peaceful evening under the stars. I like to take a picnic and sit on the grass to listen to the music."

"Your plan sounds perfect except for one thing."

"Really? I thought I had it pretty well thought out. What's wrong with it?"

"You haven't included me."

Smiling, Clare said, "How rude of me. Would you like to attend the concert with me?"

"What a great idea. Why didn't I think of that? What time?"

In a few minutes, the arrangements were made and Clare was able to hang up the phone. She didn't get out of bed right away, though. After all it was her day off. Usually she got started a little later in the morning than six o'clock, but being awakened by Kelly wasn't a bad way to begin a day. Her legs stretched under the covers, her arms sliding under her head as she stared up at the ceiling. There were worse ways to be awakened. She couldn't think of any at the moment but since meeting Kelly, her thinking processes were slightly askew anyway. She could imagine a better way to waken than hearing the sound of his voice though. He could be there beside her, his long, muscular body warm and—. Before her overactive imagination carried her any further, she shut down her tantalizing thoughts.

Since she considered she was only half crazy to

have agreed to go on seeing Kelly, she might as well go the rest of the way toward insanity and let Madeleine talk her into that silky jumpsuit she had waved in her face one day. It wouldn't be too dressy for the informal concert and would do wonders for her self-confidence, not to mention what, according to Madeleine, the white fabric and styling did for her figure. Not that she was trying to entice Kelly McGinnis. Of course not—but it never hurt for a woman to look her best.

By the time she had run some errands in the morning, visited Mrs. Hamilton at the nursing home, tried on the jumpsuit at Madeleine's after changing out of her borrowed finery, changed back into her regular clothes, and stopped off to see a realtor, she felt like a quick-change artist. When she arrived home, she had a full forty minutes to shower and get ready for the concert, so she was able to take her time.

She had accomplished a lot during the day and was looking forward to a relaxing evening after all her running around. As she blow-dried her hair, she reassessed that last thought. The stars, the music, and the clear night might prove to be relaxing, but she wasn't so sure about the man who would be with her. Kelly stirred up a lot of feelings in her, but so far, relaxation hadn't been one of them.

What the heck, she told her reflection, it had been a long time since she had done something really dumb. She was due. A few hours in his company. What could it hurt?

Even though the outdoor concert had drawn a lot of people, Kelly found a spot under a tree on a grassy knoll overlooking the bandstand, where he spread out the blanket Clare had brought. Most of the people had gathered near the gazebo-style bandstand, apparently wanting to see the music being played as well as to hear it. That was fine with Kelly. The other people were far enough down the hill to give them the feeling of semiprivacy.

After lugging the basket Clare had handed him, Kelly finally found out why it had been so heavy. She had packed a bottle of chilled wine, several types of cheese, a variety of crackers and rolls, and some fruit. There were also two ivory linen napkins, two china plates, and silverware for two.

Removing two long-stemmed glasses and the bottle of wine from the basket, he remarked, "There are more ways of gilding the lily than with powder and paint. You are what my Gran would call lace-curtain."

"Really? Why?"

Settling down onto the blanket with his long legs stretched out, he leaned on his elbow. Still holding the bottle of wine, he explained, "Some people's idea of a picnic would be a few bologna sandwiches stuffed into plastic baggies, a sack of potato chips, and a can of beans, all served on flimsy paper plates with plastic forks alongside." Gesturing to the basket of goodies she had packed, he stated, "This is definitely lace-curtain. My Gran sets great store on the niceties as she calls them. To her, only a lace-curtain lady bothers with the extras. She takes great pride in being lace-curtain Irish." He tore off a piece of cheese and popped it in his mouth.

"What other kind of Irish is there other than lace-curtain?"

Helping himself to several crackers and more cheese, he replied, "There's also shanty Irish. They like a wee dram of whisky, love to laugh, and take life as it's handed to them."

"That doesn't sound so bad to me."

Grinning up at her, Kelly agreed, "We McGinnises are a mixture of lace-curtain and shanty, changing off as it suits us." Lifting his glass of wine in a mock toast, he drawled in a brogue straight from Killarney, "Tonight I'll do me Gran proud by using me best lace-curtain manners."

In the distance they could hear the sounds of various instruments warming up as the symphony players began taking their places.

Clare placed some food on her plate and made herself comfortable. "Have you ever been to one of these concerts before?"

He didn't want to admit he hadn't even known about them. His usual encounters with women consisted of wining, dining, and bedding. Maybe it didn't show much imagination but it usually got the results he wanted.

"No, I haven't, but apparently you have."

"I came with Mrs. Hamilton the year the concerts began. She and her husband were patrons of the symphony for years. She fought with the directors of the symphony to bring the orchestra out of the symphony hall so everyone could benefit—families with children, senior citizens, people who wouldn't or couldn't attend the symphony hall. She fought them all, everyone from the mayor, the town council, and the Chamber of Commerce to the Daughters of the Confederacy, to get the support she needed. The biggest complaint was that the symphony had meager funds to support even its regular concerts, so Mrs. Hamilton raised the money to fund the outdoor concerts. Then the powers-that-be balked because there weren't accommodations large enough for the large orchestra."

"So your Mrs. Hamilton solved that problem by building the bandstand?"

"The bandstand was already here. What she did was to suggest that only half the members of the orchestra needed to participate, which would also cost less. The musicians were asked to volunteer and enough of them liked the idea to go along with it."

"Your Mrs. Hamilton sounds like an enterprising lady."

"Opposition only makes her more determined. The first outdoor concert was scheduled on a Fourth of July. The music was patriotic marches with fireworks at the finale while the symphony played "America the Beautiful." Mrs. Hamilton said there wasn't a dry eye in the place."

"She must have a flair for showmanship."

Reaching into the basket, Clare dug around and came up with a corkscrew which she handed to Kelly. "Your Gran would definitely consider her to be lace-curtain. Getting the job done was always important, but the job had to be done with style. Appearances were always important to her. The smallest detail was as important as the largest."

"You use different tenses when you talk about her. I take it she is still alive, but not actively setting the world right?"

Clare's expression became sober for a moment. "Mrs. Hamilton isn't well so she's more or less retired." She gave him a sideways glance, a slight smile curving her mouth. "You've seen a sample of how she thinks the world should be presented, with a little pizzazz, a little class, a lot of style."

"You mean the house?"

"I mean the Beautique. All her salons were designed basically like the Beautique. She wanted them to be on a grand scale so her patrons would feel special, pampered, leaving with the feeling they'd been treated like royalty."

Leveling himself into a sitting position, he pulled up his legs to place the bottle between his knees. With a few deft turns of the corkscrew, the bottle was open and he poured the wine into their glasses. "You said all her salons. How many are there?"

"There were twenty-one franchised salons scattered all over the country, when she sold out two years ago. Most of the salons kept her name to take advantage of the commercial value, but I couldn't." She looked out over the people seated on the ground or on the lawn chairs they had brought with them. "I had taken so much from her. It didn't seem right to take her name as well."

Kelly thought that was an odd comment to make but Clare didn't give him an opportunity to ask her to clarify it.

Tilting her head to look at him, she said, "I suppose that sounds silly or melodramatic but it was how I felt. I chose the name Beautique instead, but I kept the decor the way she liked it because her concept of what women wanted was a good one. Otherwise I wanted the salon to stand on its own."

The orchestra members were adjusting their music on the stands, their instruments silent as they awaited the entrance of the conductor. Kelly knew he only had a few minutes left before the music would drown out any conversation.

"Would I recognize the professional name you didn't want to take?"

"It depends on how familiar you are with women's beauty products."

"Probably as familiar as you are about carpentry tools, but try me. There are a lot of women in my family. I may have heard of your Mrs. Hamilton's alias."

"It's not an alias exactly. She used her first name, Alyssia."

To Kelly's amazement he was familiar with the name. He remembered pots of creams and lotions with *Alyssia* printed on them littering the bathroom he had shared with his sisters when he was growing up. There had been a book written about her life too. One of his sisters had devoured the darn thing from cover to cover when she was going through her Madame Curie stage, interested in inventing anything that would remove her wretched freckles.

The conductor made his entrance and mounted the podium. The moment he raised his baton, all chance of satisfying Kelly's curiosity had to be postponed. At first he was irritated because of the interruption. There were still so many questions he wanted to ask, so many things he wanted to know about Clare. Then, the air became filled with the melodic strains of one of Beethoven's concertos. Since Kelly wasn't much of an expert on classical music he had no idea which particular sonata or concerto or whatever was being played but it didn't matter. The evening air became filled with magical sounds, enchanting music, hushing the audience.

The program didn't stick only to classical pieces. There was a blend of pop, jazz, show tunes, a couple of numbers from the fifties; a little something for everyone.

When they switched to a ballad rendition of "When Irish Eyes Are Smiling," Kelly leaped to his feet and held out his hand. Laughing, Clare accepted his hand and was pulled up into his arms to be held closely against him, their feet moving slowly over the grass. The violins played the song as a plaintive melody rather than a gay tune.

Since Kelly was holding her so closely, she didn't have to speak very loudly in order for Kelly to hear her. "I think the conductor is Irish."

She could feel his mouth curve into a smile against her hair. "Why?"

"He must be homesick. Those violins are practically crying their hearts out. If they play 'Danny Boy' next, I'm liable to break down myself and I'm not even Irish. I thought you Irish were a happy bunch."

"We're an emotional bunch." He drew away from her enough to look own into her face. "Maybe he'll compensate his sad rendition with a good old Irish jig to cheer you up."

"Well, if he does, you're on your own. I've never jigged in my life."

Bringing her back into his warmth, he chuckled. "We'll have to see what we can do to change that. Now shut up, lily of my life, and let the music talk to you."

Clare relaxed against him, her thighs moving with his. The lilting violins drifted in the night air, binding them together as they danced under the stars. The vibrant feel of his strong arms and taut male body talked to her more than the tune being played. The communication between them was purely sensual, growing as the friction of their bodies heightened their awareness of each other. The magnetic pull was growing in strength, irreversible and powerful.

For now it was enough to hold each other, to let the magic flow over them, strangely content—for now.

When the last note died away, they gazed at each other for a long time and then Kelly smiled down at her, his expression warm and tender. The orchestra changed tempo and mood, swinging into a frolicking rendition of "Roll Out the Barrel" which put an end to any desire on their part to continue dancing. With a slight bow, he led her back to the blanket. He picked up the glasses of wine and handed one to her. He then clinked his with hers. Leaning back against the tree, he gently pulled her between his legs, shifting her until she was pressed into his chest. The orchestra began a slow, romantic piece.

His arms came around her, his hands clasped under her breasts to hold her loosely, yet securely. The imprint of his palm spread over her stomach branded her with heat, making it difficult for her to breathe. The lilting music filled the air around them, enclosing them in a sensual whirlpool, swirling around them in waves. She was conscious of his warmth and strength against her spine, the scent of him, the feel of his warm breath in her hair.

The night became even more magical when a bird perched in the tree above them accompanied the more sophisticated musical instruments played by the men and women in the bandstand.

As if to hold onto the enchanting night, Clare placed her hands over his. If it was up to her, the concert could go on forever.

At the end of the concert, the conductor and the orchestra took their well-deserved applause, and Kelly was amazed to discover over two hours had passed. Reluctantly, he loosened his hands and slid them across her ribcage. He didn't really want to let her go but there was no longer any reason for them to stay.

Moving away from the secure position in Kelly's arms, Clare began to gather up the remnants of their picnic. She glanced quickly over at Kelly. His expression gave her no clue to whether he had enjoyed the concert or whether he had been bored out of his skull.

"If you're waiting for an encore, you have a long wait. That was it."

He shifted onto his knees and helped her repack the basket. "I really enjoyed the concert. To be honest, I didn't think I would."

"Then why did you want to come?"

"Because this is where you were going to be." He shut the clasps on the basket and then reached over to touch her nose with the tip of his finger. "It's difficult to try to build any type of relationship if you're at a concert and I'm at a baseball game."

She smiled. "I suppose it could be done but it wouldn't be as much fun."

Kelly's hand went to the back of her neck and pulled her toward him even though the picnic basket was between them. "I can't resist a beautiful woman who likes fun." Leaning over, his mouth covered hers hungrily, taking her breath away with the intensity. "In fact I can't resist you at all. Let's go."

Kelly parked the car in front of Mrs. Hamilton's house and shut off the engine. For a moment he made no move to open his door right away. "Am I invited in?"

Turning her head slowly to look at him, she asked, "For coffee?"

His eyes remained intently on her face. "Eventually."

It was time for the decision she had known she was going to have to make before the night was over. This involvement with Kelly could cost her more emotionally than she could afford, or it could prove to be the most priceless thing in her life. An affair with him could make her joyously happy or break her heart, but she would never know unless she took the chance.

Taking a steadying breath, she stated quietly, "I make lousy coffee."

"I make terrific coffee."

"Don't tell me. Let me guess. Irish coffee, right?"

He smiled. "I can make Irish coffee but I'm a whiz at regular coffee too."

What a ridiculous conversation they were having. This isn't the way she thought affairs should start. Shouldn't he be saying sweet nothings in her ear instead of calmly discussing coffee?

Kelly smiled. He knew she was uncomfortable and found it rather endearing. He was more than ready for the next step in their relationship. He hoped she was. He opened his car door and came around to open hers. His arm settled around her waist and they walked up the steps to the front door. He stood patiently while she fumbled in her purse for the house key and took it out of her hand when she withdrew it from her purse. Lowering his head, he kissed her deeply as he slipped the key into the ornamental lock and unlocked the door. Still kissing her, he pushed open the door and drew her into the hall with him.

The phone began to ring, startling Clare out of the sensual wave crashing over her. Drawing away slowly, she murmured, "I'd better answer it."

Nodding, Kelly followed her into the living room. The soft look created by their brief kiss faded as she listened to whoever was on the phone. Her expression became grim, her eyes concerned, her mouth taut with worry. "I'll be right there," she said into the phone before hanging up.

Turning to Kelly, she said, "I'm sorry, but I have to go somewhere."

Kelly didn't waste time asking any questions. Her face said it all. Something had happened and it wasn't anything good. "I'll take you wherever you have to go."

At first she was going to refuse but he took charge, not giving her a choice. Without wasting any time, he drew her back outside, locking the door behind them and pocketing her key. In the car, he asked, "Where to?"

She gave him the directions and within twenty minutes, they arrived at the McMillon Nursing Home. If Kelly was surprised to end up at such a place, he didn't say anything. Now wasn't the time for questions. She needed his support, not the third degree. He accompanied Clare inside and waited beside her as she went up to the desk. The woman behind the desk recognized her and told her the doctor was waiting to talk to her.

Turning to Kelly, she said, "You don't have to wait for me."

"I'll be here."

"I don't know how long I'll be."

His hand cupped her neck briefly, his smile gentle and reassuring. "Go on, Lily,"

Oddly, the use of her nickname was the assurance she needed. Smiling faintly, she walked away, disappearing from view when she entered one of the rooms.

Looking around the small lobby, he found a semi-comfortable chair and sat down.

After two hours and three cups of the worst coffee he had ever drunk, Kelly saw Clare come back down the hallway. He examined her face closely. She was holding herself as though the weight of the world had descended on her shoulders, although there was definitely relief in her eyes as though things hadn't been as bad as she thought they would be.

He got up from the chair and waited for her to come to him. He had promised himself not to bombard her with questions, but he allowed himself one. "Are you all right?"

She fought the impulse to walk into his arms. She was relieved to find him still waiting for her although she really hadn't expected him to hang around so long. "I could use a cup of your terrific coffee."

Coffee was the last thing he wanted after consuming three cups of shoe polish.

Taking her arm, he drew her toward the exit. "You got it."

It felt unusual to be cosseted but it was exactly what Clare needed. When they returned to Mrs. Hamilton's house, Kelly made coffee and insisted they have it in the living room instead of the kitchen. She sat on the couch with her legs tucked under her, cupping the mug between her hands to warm them. Kelly took a chair several feet away from her, not wanting her to feel crowded in any way.

Taking a sip of coffee, Clare looked up and met Kelly's gaze.

"You were right. You do make good coffee." Her gaze dropped to the cup she held. "I want to thank you for driving me to the nursing home and staying to wait for me. You didn't have to, you know."

"I rarely do anything I don't want to do. I would like to know why you went to the nursing home."

"Mrs. Hamilton lives there."

"The Mrs. Hamilton who owned this house?"

"Yes. The nursing home called me to tell me she was ill, but she's going to be all right. The doctor thinks she suffered a slight stroke. When I went into her room, she was pale and lifeless, but the doctor explained he had given her a sedative." Her mouth curved into a wry smile. "She fights the indignities as she calls them; all the shots, the treatments, the IV's, the nurses turning her, the doctors probing and poking at her. Occasionally she has to be sedated for her own good." She sighed heavily. "Sometimes she can be so stubborn. She fights the doctors tooth and nail."

"Fighting is better than giving up."

Clare laid her head against the back of the couch. "Giving up is not in Mrs. Hamilton's vocabulary."

"You care for her a great deal, don't you?" he asked quietly.

Her eyes met his and she stated baldly, "She's my family," realizing for the first time that it was true. Seeing his eyes widen in surprise, she added, "We're not related in any way but she's been more of a family to me than my own ever was." Her eyes closed and she murmured, "I'm the only one Mrs. Hamilton has to take care of her now. She depends on me."

She was exhausted and Kelly felt more protective toward her than inquisitive. Putting down his empty mug, he got out of his chair and went over to her. Taking her mug out of her hand, he bent down and lifted her into his arms. "There's nothing you can do for her any more tonight, Lily. You need to get some sleep."

Her arms automatically went around his neck and she sighed, her breath soft and fragrant against his neck. "What time is it?"

Carrying her up the stairs, he answered, "Time for you to go to bed."

She mumbled sleepily, "This isn't exactly how I thought this evening would end."

He pushed open her bedroom door with his foot, a wry smile lifting the corner of his mouth. "Me either but I'm not complaining."

Gently he lowered her onto her bed and pulled back the covers. He removed her shoes and then unbuttoned her jumpsuit, unable to look away when he slid the silky material over her hips and down her legs, revealing her satiny skin scantily covered by a cream lace bra and panties.

His eyes slid up her body slowly and met her quiet gaze. Giving her a weak smile, he reached down and pulled the covers up to her shoulders, concealing the tempting view of her flesh while he still could.

Looking down at her, he said huskily, "I'll give you a call tomorrow."

She nodded, her eyes dwelling on his face, seeing the darkened passion tamped down in his eyes. "Our evenings never seem to turn out the way we plan."

He sat down on the edge of the bed, hip to hip. His hand reached out to touch her hair, the only part of her he dared to touch. "You have to admit it hasn't been dull. I'm willing to try again. How about you?"

"What would your Gran say about a situation like this?"

A corner of his mouth lifted. "She would tell me always to believe in the luck of the Irish. It always changes for the good."

"Always?"

He leaned down to touch her lips lightly with his, his guts tightening in a knot when he felt her mouth move under his. His breath brushed against her skin. "Always trust the luck of the Irish, me darlin'. I do." He stared down at her for a long minute. "I have to leave. You need your rest."

At the door he looked back at her, watching her as she was watching him. Then he left.

Six

While her coffee was brewing the following morning, Clare phoned the nursing home to check on Mrs. Hamilton's condition. She knew she would have been called if it had worsened during the night but she phoned anyway for reassurance. The news was good. The older woman had had a peaceful night.

Which is more than she could say about her own. When she had finally gotten to sleep, her dreams were full of leprechauns and shamrocks, all mixed up with a castle in the air and a black-haired, blue-eyed man dancing an Irish jig.

She was in trouble. Deep trouble. She was beginning to believe in Irish luck. Even worse, she was beginning to believe in one particular Irishman.

When the phone rang as she was having her second cup of coffee, she said lightly, "Top of the morning to you, Mr. McGinnis."

The sound of his rich deep laughter made her smile in response. "That's an awful Irish accent you have, Lily, but a nice try. How did you know it was me?"

"A lucky guess."

He sounded pleased. "So you're beginning to believe in Irish luck, are you?"

"I prefer to call it brilliant deduction. There aren't a lot of people I know who would be phoning me at six-thirty in the morning. I've already phoned the nursing home so I knew it couldn't be them. Unless it was an obscene phone caller or a wrong number, I figured it had to be you, especially when you seem to have this habit of calling me at the crack of dawn."

If the previous night had ended the way he had wanted, he wouldn't be phoning her at all. He'd have woken up beside her. Since he wasn't with her, he wanted to make plans to be with her. "I wanted to catch you before you went to work since I don't have much luck getting through to you at the salon," he said dryly, adding, "I have a full schedule of work today so I'm calling now to make arrangements for tonight. Can you be ready about seven?"

"For what?"

He chuckled. "For whatever the night brings. We could start out by saying we're going out to dinner and see what happens."

Clare smiled, knowing he was referring to her remark last night about how their plans seemed to go awry every time they were together. "What the heck. I feel adventurous. Seven will be fine."

"Seven it is. Odds are in our favor, darlin'. What else could possibly go wrong?"

At seven-fifteen that night, Clare was asking herself that same question with a slight variation. What had gone wrong? She had another question boiling on the back burner when Kelly hadn't arrived by seven-thirty. Where in hell was he? At seven forty-five she was checking the phone line to make sure the phone was working in case he had tried to call her. There was nothing wrong with the phone.

By eight o'clock, she had to face the facts. Mr. Kelly McGinnis had stood her up.

At two minutes after eight she ran up the stairs and tore off her silk blouse as soon as she entered her bedroom. She yanked off her skirt and threw it into her closet, kicking off her shoes, not particularly caring where they landed. Stripping off her hose and bra, she grabbed her old jeans and found her favorite oversized white shirt. The pins were briskly removed from the hairstyle she had spent a fair amount of time arranging. A number of vigorous strokes with her hairbrush didn't do much for the styling of her hair but did a great deal for her temper.

So the evening wouldn't be a complete loss, she might as well get back to the woodworking manual. The thought of bashing away with a hammer sounded very appealing at the moment.

As she was coming back down the stairs, the phone rang. At first she was going to ignore it. She wasn't in the mood to chat with anyone from the salon calling about some minor problem. Then it occurred to her it might be the nursing home, so she was compelled to answer it.

Her hello was practically drowned out by an astonishing hullabaloo. She could barely hear Kelly say her name. A child was yelling, "Is that Mommy?" and another small voice was crying in the background. She heard Kelly tell the child it wasn't Mommy and to give Mary Kate her bottle. In a few minutes there was relative quiet.

Then Kelly came back to her. "Clare? Are you still there?"

"Yes," she replied coolly. "How nice to hear from you."

He knew she would be angry and she had every right to be. "Look, I'm sorry," he said sincerely. "I tried to call you earlier but it's been a bit hectic around here."

"I gathered that from the sound effects in the background. If you're calling to tell me you won't be taking me out to dinner, I already figured that out about an hour ago."

"Well," he sighed. "Why should tonight be any different? Every time we plan something, it gets screwed up."

Sounds of discontent were starting up again in the background. She heard a heavy groan from the man on the other end of the phone and heard him speak to someone in the background, "Sean, your sister doesn't want my car keys. She wants her bottle."

Her curiosity overcame her anger. "Kelly?"

His voice came back to the phone. "Sorry. It's a zoo around here."

"I have a feeling you have a pip of an excuse for standing me up. What's going on?"

"What isn't going on? Do you remember my brother, Kevin? He was the policeman we followed to the hospital."

"I remember him." Her voice showed her sudden concern. "Has something happened to him?"

"Mr. Macho is on the policemen's softball team and the damn fool broke his ankle sliding into third base. My sister-in-law dropped their two kids off here since I was the closest relative on the way to the hospital. I was almost out the door to come for you and all of a sudden I have these two hooligans dropped in my lap. It took me awhile to calm the kids down and then I had to fix them something to eat. That's why I couldn't let you know earlier."

"I understand, Kelly. I really do." She laughed suddenly. "It's going to be a challenge to see if we can ever have an actual date."

There was a brief pause and then Kelly said, "I was hoping we could still see each other tonight if you don't mind making a few adjustments to the original plans." Then he began to explain what he had in mind.

Forty minutes later Clare parked her car near Kelly's apartment building and went around to the trunk of her car. She removed two bulky bags and used her elbow to shut the trunk lid. On her way to the entrance to his building, she realized she was smiling. No, she was grinning like an idiot. She couldn't believe she was doing this. But she was, and she was actually happy to be doing it. It was as though Kelly brought out a part of her she had never realized was there: a spontaneous, uninhibited side of her nature, eager and ready for anything.

Maybe she had suppressed this side of her nature because for so long she had been responsible for herself, for her business, and now for Mrs. Hamilton. There hadn't been any time to spare for fun. Somehow being around Kelly made her realize how much of life she had been missing.

Hefting the bags higher in her arms, she chuckled to herself. Another thing she was learning from Kelly was to be flexible.

A small boy she guessed to be around five years old opened the door when she rang the bell. He looked at her with some suspicion. "Are you Auntie Clare?"

Restraining herself from laughing at the title he had given her, she replied, "Yes, I guess I'm Auntie Clare. You must be Sean."

He nodded and opened the door wider. "Uncle

Kelly said for you to go into his bedroom. He needs the diapers."

Obeying the solemn orders, Clare started toward the bedroom. The door was ajar and she used her hip to shove it open further. Uncle Kelly was bending over a wiggling baby lying on a quilt on the bed. He had obviously changed his clothes and was wearing a pair of tight jeans and a red shirt with the sleeves rolled up. Mary Kate was, however, as naked as the day she was born.

Going over to the bed, Clare put the bags down and reached into one of them. "Sean said you needed these diapers, Uncle Kelly, but it looks like Mary Kate needs them more than you do."

He slanted a glance at her as she tore open the box of disposable diapers. "I see Auntie Clare thinks this is all very funny. If Auntie Clare doesn't hurry up, she's going to be in big trouble with Uncle Kelly."

Handing him one of the diapers, she stated in mock indignation, "Well, that's appreciation for you. Auntie Clare could have stayed home instead of doing your grocery shopping for you." She noticed how expertly Kelly was handling the diaper and Mary Kate. Uncle Kelly had done this before. "I think a thank you, Clare, would be nice."

Hauling the freshly diapered baby up into his arms, Kelly used his other arm to go around Clare's waist to pull her close. His mouth found hers in a light kiss. Lifting his head, he smiled down at her, amusement glittering in his eyes. "Thank you, Clare." His eyes darkened as his arm tightened around her, the amusement gone. "I'm glad you came."

She felt as though she was falling into a deep blue well, desire spiraling along her veins as she met his intent gaze. She relaxed against him, leaning into his strength. Her lips parted as she looked up at him and Kelly couldn't refuse her unintentional invitation. He took her mouth willingly, hungrily, as though his life depended on the sustenance he found in her.

Miss Mary Kate McGinnis had had one of her personal problems solved but apparently realized she had another discomfort, and she chose this inopportune time to notify her uncle. But then she was only fourteen months old. Uncle Kelly jumped when she used her usual way of asking for food.

When Clare's heart started to beat again, she asked, "Why is she screaming like that?"

Reluctantly loosening his hold on her waist, he sighed, "She usually has two reasons for demanding attention. Since one has been taken care of, that leaves the other problem. She's hungry."

Sean chose that moment to come running into the bedroom with a few demands of his own. Clare stood to one side as Kelly held Mary Kate with one arm and snatched Sean off his feet as he began jumping up and down on Kelly's bed. Tucking Sean under his arm as though the boy was a suitcase without a handle, Kelly headed for the door.

Over his shoulder, he said, "We'll need the other bag. Clare. Roll up your sleeves and your pant legs. It's feeding time at the zoo."

Clare stared after him. He was whistling as though he was perfectly at ease with the prospect of dealing with two small active children. In a daze, she followed him toward the kitchen.

As usual their evening plans hadn't worked out the way they were supposed to, but Clare was no longer upset. In fact she had a great time. She got a crash course on the care, feeding, and bathing of two healthy, active children. She was amazed at their energy and Kelly's ease in handling them. The children eventually wore themselves out and ended up asleep after hearing their Uncle Kelly's colorful, if inaccurate, version of *The Three Little Pigs* as they were put to bed in his bedroom, looking so tiny in his large bed. They each wore one of Kelly's shirts in place of pajamas.

Collapsing onto the couch after the children were finally asleep, Clare turned her head toward Kelly as he came into the living room after checking to make sure the children were asleep. Sitting down beside her, he propped his feet up on the coffee table.

In a lazy drawl, Clare asked, "The third little piggy lived in a townhouse?"

Kelly leaned his head back on the couch and closed his eyes. "Sean knows what sticks and bricks are but is a little shaky about straw."

Covering a wide yawn, she murmured, "You're very good with children, Uncle Kelly."

He reached out for her and pulled her over against his side, his arm holding her close. "You weren't so bad yourself, Auntie Clare."

She snuggled into his side, her hand resting on his chest, her eyes closed, enjoying his warmth and his clean male scent. "It's been an education."

Kelly smiled to himself as he remembered the look on her face when she was kneeling over the bathtub to give Mary Kate a bath. She had been fascinated as she watched the little girl splash in the water. It was obvious she hadn't much experience with children, but he got the impression she was captivated by them. His smile faded. Another woman had shown enthusiasm around children too, but it had all been an act.

He felt her slender body relax against him. Damn, she felt good. All he had to remember was that there was not going to be anything permanent with her. Their involvement was only temporary. It didn't matter if she was putting on an act or not. He wasn't getting caught in that trap again.

"Kelly?" she murmured after a period of silence.

He smiled at the drowsy tone of her voice. "What?"

"Having an affair with you isn't exactly what I thought it was going to be."

Chuckling, he tightened his hold around her. "Technically speaking, we haven't started the affair part yet."

As though she hadn't heard him, she went on, "It isn't quite what I expected. So far we haven't had any candlelight dinners. No candy and flowers. There have been no long walks on the beach, nor have we even spent much time alone."

"You've left out sex."

Tilting her head, she grinned up at him. "So have you."

Her impish smile sent heat through his veins. She had the sweetest smile. "I admit it's a serious omission on my part but it's not because of lack of intent. To be fair, there have been a few interruptions along the way."

Suddenly serious, Clare murmured, "Maybe there always will be. Maybe it's not meant to be. Have you ever thought of that?"

Shifting his long length until his back was into the corner of the couch, he brought her with him until she was partially lying over him. "It's meant to be, Lily. *We* are meant to be. We just have to work on our timing."

His hands began to move over her, his touch soothing rather than sexual. It was odd how he could be with her like this. They didn't have to talk or make love. Just being together was enough. It should scare the hell out of him to feel so comfortable with this woman but it didn't. Not any longer.

Her soft hair brushed against his skin as her head

nestled into his throat. Suddenly he was no longer feeling as comfortable as he had a moment ago. His touch was no longer soothing, but sensitive to the alluring curves under his roaming hands. The rough texture of her jeans beneath his calloused palms made him ache to feel the silky skin underneath.

His fingers moved under her shirt and slid over her bare back, and he felt the sudden intake of her breath against his throat and under his hands. He didn't resist when she shifted slightly until her weight was no longer on him but on the cushions of the couch, trapped between the back of the couch and his body. When her hips had slid over his loins, a shaft of fire tightened and burned him, forcing him to clench his teeth.

Her name came out in a groan of need and he rolled onto his side to bring his aroused body intimately into the cradle of her hips. He eased away enough to allow his hand to reach for the buttons of her shirt. Finding her breasts bare sent his blood pulsing heavily, his hand sliding over her ribcage to cover her mounded flesh.

Clare found it difficult to breathe as his fingers teased a sensitive nipple, and she gasped as he lowered his head to replace his hand with his hot mouth. She heard a soft yearning sound and vaguely realized it was coming from her own throat. Suddenly restless, her hips writhed against his, her leg sliding between his, involuntarily pressing against his aching manhood.

His breath hissed as he reacted to the simple feel of her thigh touching the part of his body that was ultrasensitive.

"Oh, God. You're burning me alive." His hips crushed her lower body into the back of the couch, pressing her leg harder against him. His harsh groan was a blend of pleasure and pain. The exquisite torture was compounded when he took her mouth almost desperately, his tongue imitating the sensuous movements of his hips.

Needing more of her, he began to remove her shirt, but the distant sound of his front door slamming and his brother calling out his name stopped him from completing what he had started. Cursing under his breath, he was off the couch and out of the room before Clare knew what had happened. He kept Kevin and his wife out in the hall for a few minutes to give her time to recover.

Clare used the time to button her shirt and pull herself together. She wasn't sure she was relieved or sorry the children's parents had arrived when they did. Her emotions and her body were too churned up to try to think rationally about anything. Running her fingers through her tangled hair, she took a deep steadying breath, wondering how long it would take her heartbeat to return to normal.

She was seated on the couch when Kelly brought Kevin and his wife, Molly, into the room. The frustration in Kelly's eyes was apparent to Clare only because she was looking closely for some sign of his reaction to their interrupted passion. She hoped her own feelings weren't obvious to his brother and sister-in-law. Kelly made it easier for Clare by taking control of the conversation, giving Kevin a hard time about his prowess on the softball field. Molly and Kevin both remembered meeting Clare at the hospital so introductions weren't necessary. Neither one appeared surprised to see her at Kelly's house. Kelly offered them something to drink but they refused. It was obvious Kevin was in pain from his injury so they didn't plan to stay. After chatting briefly, they gathered up their two sleeping children and left.

• • • •

Kelly stood in the doorway staring at Clare for the longest time, his eyes boring into her as she sat on the couch. The teasing light was gone from his eyes. The searing expression in his eyes scorched Clare with the same intensity that had heated her blood before they had been interrupted.

Clare stared back, unable to break away from his passionate gaze. She watched in fascination as a corner of his mouth lifted in a sensual smile. Slowly he raised his hand, extending it to her.

Her gaze remained locked with his as she got to her feet and went toward him. Raising her hand from her side, she felt his strong fingers close around hers. Applying a little pressure, he hauled her up against his hard length, taking her other hand instead of taking her in his arms as she had expected, bringing their joined hands alongside their legs as he had done before.

His voice was low and husky. "If I kiss you, I won't be able to let you go again. It's up to you. Do you want me to kiss you or not?"

Clare's eyes widened in surprise when she realized he was leaving the decision up to her. He had to know it would take little persuasion to make her stay after her response to his lovemaking earlier. He had to know she had no choice.

Her fingers curled tightly, almost painfully around his hands as she raised up on her toes. Without saying a word, she gave him her answer by placing her parted lips over his mouth.

For a long moment, Kelly let her have her way, accepting the tantalizing taste of her until her teeth nipped his lower lip. Then she ran her tongue over the spot to soothe any pain she might have caused.

Desire surged through him, urging his body to seek relief. The pressure of his mouth broke open her lips further to take possession of her more intimately. Tearing his hands out of her grip, his fingers went to the buttons of her shirt, opening the front to give him access to the bare flesh waiting for his touch. Her body arched when he tore his mouth from hers to seek the fullness of her breast, enclosing the swollen bud with the heat of his mouth and the roughness of his tongue.

Her blood was heating into molten lava, flowing in her veins until she thought she would explode when his hand unsnapped her jeans and loosened the zipper to make room for his hand to slip under the elastic of her panties. His hand cupped her intimately, his fingers delving into her feminine heat, burning him, burning her.

His name on her lips was a plea, an ache. "Kelly . . ."

He lifted his head from her tempting breast to look down into her glazed golden eyes, seeing the intoxicating depth of her desire for him.

His body ached to take her then. He needed to bury himself in her so badly, he was close to losing his mind. But he managed to lift her up in his arms to carry her to the couch. Taking her up the stairs to his bedroom was asking too much. It was too far. The few seconds it took to place her gently on the cushions of the couch strained his control as it was, but he couldn't brutalize her by taking her on the hard floor.

His hands swept away the barriers of their clothing, his eyes never leaving hers the whole time. He was drowning in the tawny depths of her eyes as he covered her pliant body, thrilling to the welcome he felt as her legs parted to make room for him.

The world came apart for both of them when he eased into her. They were whirled into space, out of control, holding onto each other as they plunged into the universe of passion. The tension spiraled and tightened between them, each seeking the supreme pleasure they found in every pulsing rhythmic move.

When Kelly felt the rippling tremors of her body around him, he slid his hands under her hips to hold her locked to him as he exploded into shattering fragments. His mouth absorbed her cry, and he was stunned by the immense satisfaction of knowing he had given her the same overwhelming pleasure he had received.

Slowly the world righted itself as they returned to reality. Kelly lifted his head enough to be able to look down into her eyes, astonished to see her mouth curve into a soft smile as she met his gaze.

His voice was husky as he stated, "*Now* we're having an affair."

For some reason, Clare didn't like that word as the definition of what had happened between them, but she managed to keep her feelings hidden from him. He meant they had shared a sexual experience, not a loving one. Taking her cue from him, she murmured, "You did say sex was the main ingredient."

Kelly wondered why he didn't like her using his own word back at him. It somehow wasn't the word to use for what they had shared. It had been more than sex, much more.

"So I did." He brushed several strands of damp hair away from her cheek. "Somehow I think *you're* the main ingredient."

Her eyes softened. Lifting her hand, she let her fingers trail down his strong jaw. "*We* are the main ingredient. It takes two to have an affair, doesn't it?"

He was becoming irritated with that word. He shifted off of her onto his side. "I have a very comfortable big bed upstairs with more than enough room for two. Will you stay the rest of the night?"

It was odd that she thought sharing a bed with

him for the rest of the night was too intimate, considering what they had already shared, but it was the way she felt. "No, I'd better go home."

"Why?"

Suddenly restless, she sat up and began to gather her clothing from the floor. "I didn't plan to stay the night."

His hand reached out to stall her by grabbing her arm. "You didn't plan what happened a few minutes ago either but you enjoyed it. You might enjoy sleeping with me too."

Slipping her arm into the sleeve of her shirt, she didn't even try to disagree with him. Instead she continued dressing and stated, "We agreed not to make demands on each other, if I remember our earlier agreement. We agreed not to crowd each other. You're crowding me. No commitments, remember?"

Sitting up, he picked up his jeans and put them on. "I'm not offering a commitment, only a bed for the night," he said with irritation.

"And I'm going home," she stated firmly, hoping the panic she felt wasn't evident in her eyes.

"I don't like the idea of you driving home alone at this time of night. I'll drive you home."

"No. I don't want you to drive me home."

"Dammit, Clare. Why are you being so damn stubborn?"

"It isn't stubbornness. It's being independent. You were the one who insisted we be independent when we discussed the rules of our relationship."

Fury built up in him like dynamite and exploded. "The hell with those rules!"

By now she was fully dressed except for one shoe which she was having difficulty finding. She needed to get out of there, away from him, so she could think about what had happened between them. Somehow she had gotten more than she had bargained for and she had to figure out what it meant. She was down on her knees looking under the couch for her shoe when a rustle of clothing indicated Kelly was also getting dressed.

Finding her shoe under an end table, she put it on and turned back to face him. He was wearing his jeans and had slipped on his shirt although he had left it open. He was standing with his legs slightly apart, his hands on his lean hips in an aggressive stance.

"I'd really like you to stay, Clare."

"And I'd really like to go home, Kelly."

It was obvious he didn't like her answer, but he knew she was adamant about leaving. Maybe it was for the best after all. He had some serious thinking to do and he certainly couldn't think around her.

"When will I see you again?"

Clare met his gaze and saw a strange expression in his eyes. Was he as bewildered by all this as she was? She didn't dare stay to find out. Moving quickly toward the door, she fished out her car keys. "I don't know, Kelly. Let's take this a day at a time."

When she opened the door, she turned and saw him standing in the doorway of the living room. He wasn't going to try to stop her from leaving but she thought she saw something like regret in his eyes.

Kelly stood in the living room doorway for a long time. Suddenly he slumped against the door frame and leaned his head back against the wood, his eyes closed.

Dear heaven, he hadn't wanted her to leave. He wanted her in his bed next to him, under him, over him, together. What he had thought he wanted had been to possess her body but now he realized that wasn't enough. He wanted all of her.

He had thought his obsession for her would be extinguished by making love with her, but he knew it hadn't worked. He was more obsessed than ever.

Somehow those damn rules she kept harping on were going to have to be changed.

Seven

Kelly wasn't able to talk to Clare to try to change her mind about the rules of their relationship. Not on Friday or on Saturday. The reason he couldn't talk to her was because he couldn't find her.

She didn't answer her phone at home no matter what hour of the day or night he called. On Friday, the irritatingly efficient receptionist at the salon had informed him that Miss Denham was not available. When he went to the salon, he learned the receptionist was right. Clare wasn't there. He resorted to phoning the McMillon Nursing Home on the off chance she was visiting Mrs. Hamilton, but she wasn't there either. On Saturday, she still hadn't shown up at the salon, nor was she at home when he drove out to the house looking for her.

Panic gnawed at him. Where in hell was she? Was she all right? Did she regret what had happened between them? He gave in to the sickening dread that she had been in an accident on the way home from his place and phoned the local hospital, but Clare Denham was not in their records.

Dammit! Where was she?

According to those blasted rules, he had no right to interfere in her life. They were supposed to be independent of each other. They were supposed to go merrily down their own paths except when they met occasionally as lovers. Well, it wasn't enough. Not now.

In addition to being concerned about her, he was angry as hell to be put through the torture of worrying about her. He didn't want to worry about her. No matter how he had berated himself for breaking his own vow of noninvolvement, he was already deeply involved.

By Saturday afternoon, his temper wasn't improved when he had a flat tire on the gravel road driving back from checking her house. To make his day complete, he skinned his knuckles when the tire wrench slipped as he was removing a lug nut. The country air turned blue around him as he let out his frustrations with a choice selection of curses both Irish and English.

After he had gone back to his place to change his dusty clothes and to clean the blood from his hand, he drove to The Emerald Isle. The bar was set up to resemble a pub complete with dart board, beamed ceilings, and hunting prints on the walls. They served ice with drinks only when it was asked for. The best Irish whiskey and Guinness stout were available and there were English ales on tap. The bar was also the McGinnis family's 'local,' their favorite place to have a drink or a meal when the notion struck them.

Kelly acknowledged greetings from several patrons and nodded to the barkeeper as he made his way to the back of the pub. As he expected, his father was seated at his usual table in the corner, a pint of bitter in front of him. He was regaling Kelly's brother Daniel with one of his many tall tales and having a fine time in the telling as usual.

Daniel spotted Kelly first and used his foot to shove the empty chair next to him away from the table so Kelly could sit down. When Michael McGinnis looked up to see his son approach the table, his sharp eyes noticed the less-than-happy expression on Kelly's face.

"Well, me bucko," he greeted his son, who slumped down in the captain-style chair. "You look as though you need a drink." Raising his hand, he held up his glass as a waitress finished serving a nearby table. "Make it two, lass."

Kelly changed his father's order. "I'll have a whiskey, Fiona."

His father's eyes narrowed. "A whiskey, is it? The day's been that good, has it?"

"I've had better."

It was Daniel who noticed the condition of Kelly's hand. "What's the other guy look like?"

Puzzled by the question, Kelly glanced at his brother and caught Daniel's examination of the raw skin covering his knuckles. "It was a run-in with a gravel road, not someone's jaw. I had a flat tire."

"It has to be more than a flat tire to make you look like a whipped puppy dog, Kelly," offered Daniel, adding with a broad grin and a nudge at his father's arm on the table. "I think our Kelly has a bigger problem than a flat tire, Pop."

The elder McGinnis gave Kelly a look as thorough as an X ray. He waited until Fiona brought him a fresh pint and took a healthy swig before addressing his son. "Is it true?"

Staring at the glass of whiskey Fiona had set down in front of him, Kelly growled, "Is what true?"

Daniel grinned. "Only one thing can put that look on a man's face. A woman. Is it the one you brought to the hospital?"

Michael McGinnis leaned forward, his blue eyes

sparkling with interest. "You brought a girl to the hospital the night little Patrick was born? Why didn't you introduce me to her, Kelly McGinnis? Where are your manners?"

"You were too busy running the hospital, Pop. Kevin had to retrieve you from the nurses' lounge when Patrick was born, if you'll remember. There wasn't an opportunity to introduce Clare to you when you were roaming all over the place."

"So her name is Clare, is it? She's the one tying you up in knots?"

Kelly tossed back the whiskey. "Slip knots, square knots, and granny knots," he admitted with a twisted smile.

His father nodded his head knowingly and leaned back in his chair. "They can do them all," he said sagely. "They learn how to tie those knots from the moment they draw their first breath. It's up to us to untie them. What puzzles me is why you're here instead of out there untying knots."

In a low voice, Kelly mumbled, "I can't find her."

Both Daniel and his father leaned forward at the same time. "You what?" they asked in unison.

"I can't find her," he said in disgust.

The other two McGinnises exchanged looks, their eyes full of devilish amusement. It was Daniel who brought his gaze back to his brother first, asking calmly, "You mean she's lost somewhere?"

"I mean I can't find her. It's as though she's disappeared into thin air."

"When did you last see her?"

"Last night." He looked up from his empty glass and saw how his father and brother were trying to keep from laughing. "It's not funny!"

His father had to disagree. "It is, you know, Kelly me boy. I haven't seen you in such a fit of sulking since you were nine and the Little League coach made you sit on the bench because you used a curse word when you were struck out. I must say I'm pleased it's a woman causing you to act like a lion with a thorn in its paw. I wish I had met this Clare. She must be quite an exceptional lady to have you in such a dither." Ignoring the scowl from Kelly, he continued, "Either order yourself another drink to drown your sorrows or go find your lady. It isn't like you to sit on your duff if there's something you want and it's obvious you want this one."

Scraping back his chair, Kelly levered his "duff" out of the chair and met his father's faded blue eyes. "You're right, Pop. I want this one. I'll see you all later."

Clare had to concentrate to keep the car on the road as she returned home early Sunday morning. Exhaustion hung heavily on her shoulders and made her eyes difficult to focus, her natural reflexes almost nonexistent, her senses dull with fatigue. Going without sleep for two nights and having the added burden of financial worries had used up her resources of strength. She was operating on automatic pilot as she drove up the lane to Mrs. Hamilton's house. What kept her going was the thought of a quick shower and her bed.

It took her tired mind a few seconds to recognize there was something out of place in the driveway in front of the house. A large black object was in her way so she parked her car behind it. Staring ahead, she realized it was Kelly's Blazer. It appeared to be empty.

Getting out of her car, she looked around, wondering where he was. Puzzled, she happened to glance through the window as she walked by his car and she stopped suddenly. Opening the door on the driver's side, she climbed up onto the seat, turning toward the back. The man lying in the back was sound asleep. The back seat had been lowered to give him more room to stretch out in. A folded soft leather jacket served as a pillow. He was dressed in jeans and a heavy white sweater, his male form radiating his strength and virility even in sleep.

Clare felt an absurd tightness in her chest. Just the sight of him was oddly comforting, giving her an odd feeling of security just because he was there. It was ridiculous but the feelings flowed deep inside her, soothing her fears. She didn't know why he was asleep in his car in front of her house but she was glad he was there. Just the sight of him lifted the heavy burden of responsibility, had eased the weight of feeling so alone.

She couldn't just leave him sleeping in the truck. Reaching out, she shook Kelly's shoulder and called his name softly. The second time she called out his name and shook him she finally got a response. It was more of a muffled grunt than an outright word she could make any sense out of so she shook him again.

"Kelly! Wake up!"

He coiled his long frame in the space behind the two front seats, instantly awake. He whirled around to face her, crouched low in the limited space.

"Where in hell have you been?" he demanded with a great deal of irritation and no sign of sleepiness.

She was so startled by the unexpected attack all she could do was stare at him. On top of the strain of the last couple of days, his anger was too much to face in her exhausted state. She felt the tears of fatigue and disappointment well up in her eyes and she retorted, "If all you can do is yell at me, you can just leave."

He had seen the way she flinched when he attacked her verbally. Now he noticed the dark violet shadows under her eyes and the tears shimmering in their golden depths. His voice softened but not his intent. "I was waiting for you. For two days. Where have you been?"

She was too tired, too unprepared to face his anger. Abruptly, she turned away and climbed back down out of the Blazer onto the ground. He could darn well rot in his stupid truck. She was going to take a shower and then lose herself in the blessed oblivion of sleep.

Kelly hadn't spent the night sleeping in his car just to let her simply walk away from him now. He caught up to her as she was unlocking the front door with the spare key she had to use since she couldn't find her other key, unaware that Kelly still had it. He immediately saw how completely exhausted she was. She was slumping against the frame of the door as if for support as she fumbled with the key in the lock. It was then he noticed she was wearing the same clothes she'd had on when she'd left his place Thursday night. Wherever she had been had been rough on her and had happened shortly after she had left him.

Brushing her hand away, he unlocked the door and opened it. He lifted her up in his arms, kicking the door shut behind them with his foot after he carried her over the threshold. Without any hesitation, he headed for the stairs, carrying her easily. The door to her bedroom was open and he walked directly to her bed, laying her gently down.

As if through a haze, she watched him as he removed her shoes, then sat on the bed beside her. She was aware enough to know he wasn't planning on a seduction scene. There was no desire in his eyes as he looked down at her, only concern and tenderness. The anger of a few minutes ago had disappeared. When he asked her a question, it seemed to come from a long distance away and she mumbled, "What?"

"Where's your nightgown?"

Her hand felt like a lead weight as she lifted it to point toward a dresser. "Top drawer. Left-hand side."

Following her directions, Kelly reached in and pulled out a peach piece of satin which matched the description she had given him the other morning on the phone. The satin slipped through his fingers, reminding him of how soft and cool Clare's skin had felt under his hands until she had become heated with passion. He had to stop that kind of thinking.

When he turned around, he saw she was attempting to sit up. She moved as though it required a great deal of effort to shift her legs over the side of the bed.

Crossing to the bed, he asked quietly, "Where do you think you're going?"

"I need a shower." She got to her feet, weaving slightly. "I've been in these same clothes for three days."

The flimsy nightwear fell to the floor as his hands automatically reached for her. Her hands came up to hold onto him because her legs had the strength of Jell-o and failed to support her weight.

Kelly pulled her into his arms to hold her against his chest, his jaw tightening as he felt her slight weight lean helplessly against him. Easing her back on the bed, he again sat down beside her. His fingers were light and gentle as he brushed her hair back from her face but there was a desperate quality in his voice as he asked softly, "What in hell have you done to yourself?"

"I'm not going to get a shower, am I?" she murmured wearily.

He shook his head. "You can't even stand. The

shower can wait. Please, honey, tell me what happened to you."

Whether it was the soft endearment, her exhaustion, or the stress of the last two days, her chest felt tight with emotion and she was afraid she was going to cry. Swallowing with difficulty, she managed to say, "Mrs. Hamilton was taken to the hospital on Thursday night. The phone was ringing as I came in the door . . . after I left you. I've been with her since then."

"Will she be all right?"

"I . . . don't know. The doctor said she was holding her own. This time it was kidney failure and she's going to require dialysis." She closed her eyes and gave a ghost of a laugh. "At least I don't have to rent the limo any more." A tear slipped from beneath her lashes as she whispered, "Oh, God. Where am I going to get the money to pay for everything?"

His hand stilled in her hair and he stared down at her, his face registering shock.

He heard her take a deep shuddering breath. She turned her face toward his hand as though seeking his warmth. He didn't move his hand. In fact he couldn't move at all. Her words had frozen him. As he continued to look down at her pieces began falling into place in his mind.

The limo, the ten-year-old Sadie, the land leased to a greenhouse and for garden plots, the do-it-yourself carpentry, all made more sense now. Clare was supporting Mrs. Hamilton. To what extent he didn't know, but he could make an educated guess it was more than she could afford, both financially and emotionally. The responsibility for caring for the elderly woman was obviously taking a heavy toll on Clare.

Her exhaustion had taken over completely. Looking down at her, he saw she had fallen into a deep sleep. With great care, he eased his hand away from her. There was nothing he could do right now about the situation regarding Mrs. Hamilton but he could ensure Clare received the rest she badly needed. He unbuttoned her shirt and gently lifted her to remove it, afraid he would wake her, but she was limp and helpless as he slipped her shirt off. Then his fingers went to the zipper of her jeans so he could slide them down over her slim hips and long legs. For a second he considered dressing her in the bit of peach silk but decided he might disturb her too much by moving her. He allowed himself one last look at the lovely sight of her, bare except for the bit of silk covering her femininity. While he fought the tormenting ache of wanting her, he brought the folded quilt from the foot of the bed up to cover her. She remained still, her breathing slow, her lovely hair spread out on the white pillowcase.

Bending down, he picked up the scrap of silk he had dropped earlier and was disgusted with himself when he realized his hand was shaking with the desire to see her delicious body clothed in the sexy slip of cloth. He folded it carefully and put it back into the drawer. He closed the drapes to darken the room and unplugged the phone. With one last lingering gaze down at her sleeping form, he left her bedroom.

Coming out of her deep sleep was a slow, disorienting process for Clare. She felt relaxed and pleasantly drowsy as she stretched her legs and arched her spine, reluctant to leave the cozy nest under the covers. Just a few minutes more and then she would get up. That's funny, she thought idly. For some reason she couldn't roll over when she tried. There was a weight on her waist holding her on her back.

Opening her eyes, she blinked several times as she pushed the remnants of sleep away and looked down at her waist under the quilt. A tan arm was lying across her and she jerked her head sideways on the pillow. Either she was dreaming, or Kelly McGinnis was in bed with her. Asleep.

She stared at his tousled dark hair and the tan shoulder exposed above the quilt. What in the world was he doing there? Fragments of memory came back of arriving home and finding Kelly in her driveway. He had been asleep then too. It seemed to be her lot in life to wake him up when he was sleeping in places he shouldn't be.

Her hand raised to his shoulder and she shook him several times. When his dark lashes lifted and blue eyes met hers, she stopped and withdrew her hand.

Clare's heartbeat accelerated as she saw awareness change his eyes to a deeper blue. Then amusement glittered in their depths and his mouth curved into a slow, lazy smile.

His voice was husky from sleep as he drawled, "You need lessons on how to wake a man."

Since his hand was skimming over her naked waist and over her ribcage, she was finding it difficult to concentrate on what he was saying. Knowing she was asking for trouble, she asked softly, "What would you suggest?"

Propping himself up on his elbow, he looked down at her. "There are several options, each better than shaking a man's shoulder like a rattle." His fingers lightly circled the tips of her breast. "You could use those soft hands to stroke my skin." He bent his head and let his tongue brush across her bottom lip, his smile acknowledging the way her tongue automatically came out to meet his. "If you kissed me anywhere on my skin, I could guarantee I would want to be awake to appreciate it."

Clare was unaware of the look of hunger entering her eyes, turning them into miniature caldrons of gold. Attempting to change the intimate direction he was taking, she murmured, "Wouldn't an alarm clock accomplish the same thing?"

His soft chuckle was low and full of sensuality. "No, honey. An alarm clock wouldn't accomplish the same thing at all." His hands deftly plucked her off the mattress and she was settled on top of his long length, her breasts crushed on his chest, his male reaction clearly evident against her lower body.

Amazing them both by taking the initiative, Clare let her lips tease his lightly with butterfly kisses over the contours of his mouth. "Is this better?"

"Definitely." His hands clasped her hips to press her into his aroused body, groaning when she responded by arching and writhing her lower body and legs. "However," he rasped thickly. "There are some reflex actions involved in this type of procedure."

"I noticed."

The temptation of her flesh caused his hands to stroke her thighs and shapely buttocks. "I'm not complaining, you understand." Switching their positions quickly, he looked down at her. "In fact, I could stand waking up this way every morning."

That sounded like a commitment of sorts, but before Clare could think more about what he had said, he kissed her. A kiss was such a tame word for what his mouth did to hers. His tongue invaded, his lips persuaded, and the combination was devastating. The pace of his lovemaking accelerated as his hands explored and paid homage to the fascinating textures and curves under his palms.

It was impossible for her to withstand the rush of exultation flowing through her veins. She had always thought she was alive. For twenty-four years, her heart had beat, her lungs had allowed her to breathe, her blood had coursed through her veins. But with Kelly, she was alive, really truly alive for the first time in her life.

Her body was something she had always taken for granted. She bathed it, clothed it, fed it. Under his touch, her skin became sensitized like the air during an electrical storm. Something inside her coiled, heated, magnetized, and became more his than hers.

A wisp of silk was the only obstacle between them and Kelly removed it deftly and expertly. Unable to wait any longer to claim her, he parted her legs and slowly eased his throbbing flesh into her feminine heat. Wanting to extend the glorious sensations spiraling along his spine, he moved against her with deliberate slowness.

Clare thought she would dissolve with pleasure. Wanting to give him a portion of the pleasure he was giving her, she raised her hands to his shoulders and then across his muscular back, bringing her breasts more fully in contact with his chest as he moved against her. She was rewarded by a deep moan reverberating through his chest.

Together they rode out the passion, reaching for the summit of supreme satisfaction waiting for them just beyond the heaven they were finding in each other's arms.

As she neared the edge, Clare called out his name. "Kelly!"

"I've got you, honey. Hang on to me."

With one last surge, they fell over the precipice together.

Later, when their heartbeats had returned to normal, Clare lay with her head on Kelly's shoulder. She had needed the intense lovemaking with Kelly, not only because of the needs of her body but as a confirmation of living. During the last two days at Mrs. Hamilton's bedside as the older woman held on to life with a frail but stubborn will, Clare had been made aware of the inevitability of the loss of a friend. Being with Kelly had brought her comfort and she lay close to him, relaxed and at peace.

But it didn't last.

Kelly's fingers lingered in the strands of her hair. "Clare?"

Amusement lightened her voice. "I'm still here."

Even though he knew she was waiting, he didn't speak right away. When he finally did, he asked, "Why didn't you call me?"

She lifted her head, puzzled by the question and his tone. "When?"

His eyes were unusually serious. "When you were notified about Mrs. Hamilton or while you were at the hospital, why didn't you call me?"

It hadn't occurred to her to call him or anyone else. She didn't know what to say except the truth. "I didn't think of it."

The truth hurt. It really hurt. He had expected those exact words but they still hurt. A finger lifted to trace along her jaw. "You had the right to call me, you know. For anything. At any time. I would have come."

Her lashes hid her eyes as she lowered her gaze to her hand on his chest. "Kelly," she began hesitantly. "I—"

He saved her from explaining by stating roughly, "You aren't used to leaning on anyone but yourself, are you? You never thought of me at all."

The harsh accusation cut into her and she didn't think before she spoke in her defense. "That's not true," she said strongly. "Thinking about you was the only thing that kept me going during the long, lonely hours of waiting to learn whether or not Mrs.

Hamilton was going to make it through the night, the next day, and the next night." Realizing how much she had revealed, she pulled away from him, sliding off the bed. Hurrying to her closet, she withdrew a white terry robe and slipped it on, tying the belt around her waist. She needed to distance herself from him suddenly. Cold reality had replaced the warm glow of their lovemaking.

There were sounds of movement behind her, the creaking of the springs in her bed and the rasping slide of a zipper. Taking her courage in both hands, she turned to face him. Dressed in his jeans, he was shrugging on his shirt, his eyes on her.

Holding her gaze, he said quietly, "We need to talk."

She knew what he wanted to talk about. She had just broken their agreement about noninvolvement by her confession. Nodding, she moved toward the door. "I'll make some coffee."

He caught up with her at the door. "*We'll* make coffee. You're no longer a solo act."

Without the faintest idea what that last remark meant, Clare was silent as she left her bedroom and went down the stairs with Kelly beside her.

In the kitchen, Kelly asked, "When was the last time you had something to eat?"

"I—don't remember. What time is it now?"

"It's a little after seven. In the evening. And it's Sunday."

"I do know what day it is," she said huffily, although to be honest, she really hadn't been sure. For the life of her, she couldn't remember when she had eaten last. She had gone to the hospital coffee shop once while Mrs. Hamilton was being examined by one of the specialists but she had only managed to choke down half a chicken sandwich along with a cup of bitter coffee.

Kelly opened the refrigerator and took out a carton of eggs, which was about all he found inside. "You make the coffee and I'll fix us some eggs. I hope you like them scrambled because that's the only way I can cook them."

Rummaging around in her cupboards, he found a can of Spam and sliced the block of meat. In a short time, he had prepared the eggs and fried the Spam, and Clare had toasted some bread. She poured the coffee and they sat down at the table in the alcove to eat the combination breakfast, lunch, and supper.

Kelly waited until she had eaten every speck of food off her plate before he bluntly took up from where they had left off in her bedroom.

"I meant what I said, Clare. You have the right to ask me for anything. Not just in bed but at any time. I assumed you knew that but apparently you have to have it spelled out for you."

"That wasn't part of our agreement."

Biting back his opinion of what could be done with the stupid agreement they had made, he stated, "The original arrangement was made before we became lovers and was dissolved after we became lovers. What happens between us is more than two people indulging in a brief affair and you know it." He pushed his plate to one side and rested his arms on the table, his eyes drilling into her, daring her to dispute what he had said.

She wasn't able to contradict him. It was how she felt, but what amazed her was that he admitted to feeling the same way about the restrictions they had made. "So where do we go from here?" she asked quietly.

"The agreement we made before no longer exists. Let's forget sensible arrangements about not getting involved. We *are* involved, Lily. I don't know for how long, but right now we've started something and we have to see where it goes."

She noticed he was still putting limits on their relationship by his last remark, as though he didn't expect their alliance to last. He was still playing it safe by not committing to anything but an affair, but it was too late for her to protect herself from being involved. Her heart had made a commitment she was afraid would be impossible to eradicate.

Kelly watched her lower her gaze to the table, making it impossible for him to see her eyes, shutting him out. His hand came across the table to take hers. "Clare, look at me."

He saw the way she stiffened her spine as though preparing herself for a firing squad. Slowly she raised her eyes to meet his but he was unable to read anything in her expression. He wished he knew what was going through her mind.

"Do you want to see where this leads or not?"

Clare was wondering the same thing. Did she want to continue seeing him, with the hope their relationship could develop into something permanent, along with the fear he might decide otherwise? She gave him the only answer she could give. "I don't know, Kelly. I have a lot of other things to think about right now and I—"

"And one of them is how you're going to pay Mrs. Hamilton's medical bills."

"How—how do you know that?"

"Something you said last night. It's true, isn't it? You've been supporting Mrs. Hamilton. That's why you're selling the house and counting all the pennies you get from the lease of the garden plots." His voice changed slightly, a hard edge of anger apparent as he added, "And why you've been experimenting with hammers and saber saws to save on the cost of carpentry repairs."

Wearily, Clare propped her elbow on the table and rested her forehead in her hand. "I'd rather not talk about my problems, if you don't mind."

His eyes narrowed. "Why not?"

"Because they're *my* problems."

Kelly felt like a door had just been shut in his face. She would share her body but not her problems. It wasn't enough.

Remembering his Gran's warning about pushing ahead too fast, Kelly didn't press her for answers she wasn't ready to give. She was under enough pressure right now. He wasn't going to add to them. At least not yet.

"Will you do something for me?"

She frowned and asked cautiously, "What?"

He stood up and came around the table. He reached down to bring her up to stand in front of him. His hands cupped her face. The apprehension in her eyes was quite apparent. In a sober tone, he asked, "Will you wash the dishes? I'll dry them but I hate washing the darn things."

Surprise quickly changed to laughter. No matter how things turned out between them, Clare would remember how Kelly could always make her laugh. He made the sun brighter, the moon fuller, and the air clear and clean whenever he was with her.

His hand came under her chin. For several minutes, he looked down at her. "Take everything one day at a time, Lily. Your financial worries, Mrs. Hamilton, and me. Okay?"

Her hand came up to cover his. "Okay."

Suddenly he lifted her up in his arms. "Forget the dishes," he said as he carried her out of the kitchen toward the stairs. "I'll do them later. I believe you said something about wanting a shower." Taking the stairs easily holding her securely in his arms, he grinned down at her. "I'll introduce you to an Irish shower."

Laughing up at the face so close to her own, Clare asked, "Will I turn green?"

His eyes looked down at her, amusement blending with stark sensuality. "Don't make light of an ancient ritual."

There was a great deal of skepticism in her voice. "How could it be an ancient ritual? Showers haven't been around all that long. How old is this ancient ritual supposed to be?"

"As old as time," he murmured against her lips, lowering her legs so she could stand on the tiled floor in the bathroom. His fingers deftly loosened the tie around her waist. The robe parted and Kelly couldn't resist the rosy flesh exposed to his gaze and hands.

"And very basic," he muttered hoarsely as his rough palms closed over her hips to bring her into his fevered body.

Clare managed to whisper, "Oh, *that* ancient ritual," just before his mouth closed urgently over hers, ending any further conversation and starting the tempest in her blood.

Eight

In the early hours of the following morning, Kelly dressed quietly and left Clare asleep in her bed. It was still dark outside, with early morning dew on the ground. He could feel the cool dampness on the doorknob as he let himself out of the front door, shutting it quietly behind him.

For some ridiculous reason, he disliked leaving the house like a thief. No matter how practical it was to go home to shower and change his clothes before going to work, he didn't like it. It was funny. It had never bothered him before. Thinking back, he couldn't recall a single incident when he had felt any reluctance to leave a warm woman in bed after a night of pleasure. The women he had dated after his divorce had been forgotten the moment he left their beds. He had gotten on with his life and had expected them to get on with theirs with no regrets, no recriminations.

It wasn't the same with Clare. Hell, he thought grimly. Nothing was the same with Clare. Making love with her was like nothing he had ever experienced before, making him realize exactly what that phrase actually meant. He had used those words as a description of the sexual act before but had been wrong. With other women, he had had sex. With Clare, he had made love. There was a hell of a big difference between the two.

Sitting behind the wheel of the Blazer, he stared at the dark outline of the old house. No matter how he tried to ignore its aging beauty, he recalled the moments he had found himself thinking of various improvements and embellishments as he had wandered around the house while Clare slept. His hands would brush over the smooth banister and lovingly stroke the walnut doors in passing—until he realized what he was doing. Then he would jerk away as though the wood had burned his flesh. After losing his own house, he had vowed never to become attached to another building, but when he realized he hated the thought of anyone else living in Mrs. Hamilton's home, he had to admit the house was getting to him.

So was the woman who was asleep in one of the bedrooms.

At noon, Clare was getting her purse out of her desk prior to leaving the salon when she looked up to see Kelly in the doorway of her office. She wasn't aware of the pleasure glowing in her eyes at the sight of him as he leaned against the door frame. Dressed in a pair of khaki slacks and a white shirt with tiny tan lines, he looked casually elegant as he held a brown jacket slung over his shoulder by one finger.

She was immaculately attired in her 'work' clothes. The brown dress was almost the same color as her hair and could have made her look like a dull brown sparrow, but the boldly patterned, colorful scarf draped over her shoulders and around her neck turned her into a peacock. Her makeup had been artfully applied as usual, her hair skillfully arranged.

She looked aloof and unapproachable except for her eyes. They were warm and inviting as her gaze lingered on him. "Hi," she murmured softly.

The warmth of her smile did odd things to his breathing. "Hi. Are you ready?"

She quickly searched her memory but couldn't remember anything being said about meeting during the day. "Ah—I was going to the hospital to see Mrs. Hamilton."

"That's what I figured. I'll drive you."

"You don't have to drive me, Kelly. It would take up too much of your time."

"It's my time," he stated calmly.

Clare couldn't very well argue with that. It was just that she had to be careful not to depend on him, to lean on him. She had to remember it wasn't what he wanted. She tried again to talk him out of driving her to the hospital. "I have to be back by one-thirty."

"Then we'd better get going."

Clare gave up. He was about as flexible as a brick wall, she thought with resignation as she clutched her purse and came away from her desk. If he wanted to waste his time driving her to the hospital and back, it was obvious she couldn't stop him.

During the next hour, Kelly accomplished the two things he had set out to do. The first was to let his presence show her she didn't have to deal with Mrs. Hamilton's problems alone. The second was to find out the extent of Clare's financial obligations regarding the older woman's care.

While he was driving her to the hospital, he learned Mrs. Hamilton's medical insurance was no longer valid once she sold her businesses, due to an over-sight, a very costly oversight. Because of the compli-cated negotiations with the various buyers, the legal paperwork, and her illness, Mrs. Hamilton had ne-glected to contact her insurance company to take out a policy apart from the group insurance pre-viously arranged through her business. Once she was no longer a part of the company, her medical insurance had been cancelled.

After seeing Mrs. Hamilton for about twenty min-utes, Clare came back to the waiting room and told Kelly that the older woman would be transferred back to the nursing home the following day. She would require round-the-clock nursing care and would need to return to the hospital regularly for dialysis treatments.

In his mind, Kelly tallied up the cost of ambu-lances to transport Mrs. Hamilton back and forth, the extensive nursing care, the cost of the hospital room, doctors' bills, fees at the nursing home, medi-cations, and dialysis. Coming up with a staggering rough estimate, he wondered how Clare had been able to keep up with the enormous bills that must be crowding her mailbox.

Walking back through the mall with Clare, they were passing an expensive dress shop with elegantly attired mannequins in the window when Kelly was reminded of the first time he had seen Clare. With a hand on her arm, he stopped their progress and drew her to stand in front of the window.

Clare glanced up at Kelly with a puzzled frown and then looked at the dresses in the window. "I doubt if they have anything in your size."

He continued to gaze at the silk suit draped over the emaciated mannequin. "The first time I ever saw you, you were wearing a suit very similar to this one."

"The first time I met you, I was wearing slacks and a blouse."

Shaking his head, he finally looked away from the suit that had caught his eye and looked down at her, a slight smile curving his mouth. "That was the first time I met you, not the first time I saw you."

Leaning against the glass, she crossed her arms in front of her. "Really? Then when was the first time you saw me?"

"I was calmly having lunch on a Wednesday last month when I looked out the window and saw you getting out of a long gray limousine in front of Chez Madeleine. I thought you were stunning but a bit rich for my blood." His smile deepened at the look of astonishment widening her eyes. "Then while I was drinking my coffee, I happen to glance out the window again and saw you coming back out of the boutique a different woman from the one who went in. You had changed into a pair of jeans and a sweater, still stunning but in a completely different way."

"I can explain all that."

"I'm not sure I want you to. I was enjoying the mystery behind your change from princess to pauper."

She told him anyway. "I went through the charade for Mrs. Hamilton. She would have been terribly upset if she thought I was having any financial difficulties. It seemed kinder to let her go on thinking all the plans she had made for my future were working out. The woman was depressed enough with her debilitating illness. She didn't need any added grief."

"I figured it had something to do with Mrs. Hamilton." He lifted his hand and slowly touched her face. "When I saw you coming out of the shop that first time, you were no longer too rich for my blood, but you were in my blood. You still are."

"Kelly," she began, not sure what she wanted to say.

An elderly lady coming out of the dress shop bumped into Kelly and he automatically reached out to steady her. The woman jerked away from Kelly as if he was about to accost her and went on her way glancing nervously over her shoulder several times.

Grinning down at Clare, Kelly took her hand and continued walking in the direction of the salon. "I think we should continue this at another time."

"And another place."

At the entrance of the salon, Kelly stopped and asked, "Do you plan to see Mrs. Hamilton tonight?"

"No. The trip from the hospital to the nursing home will wear her out tomorrow. She'll be needing all the rest she can get tonight."

"Do you plan to see me tonight, then?"

She gave him a small smile. "Kelly, I've discovered it doesn't do any good to plan anything where you're concerned." Her voice took on a bewildered note, "Things just sort of happen with you."

A devilish gleam entered his eyes. "Yes, they do, don't they. I'm not complaining about some of them though. Are you?"

Clare wasn't about to answer his question. Glancing at her watch, she exclaimed, "Oh, gosh! Is that the time? I have to get back to work."

Kelly laughed. "Coward. I'll see you tonight. What time are you through here?"

"Five."

"I'll be here at five."

"And then what? A dinner we don't eat, a movie we don't see?"

"It's a surprise." He began walking away. "I'll see you at five."

•　•　•

The surprise was indeed a surprise. Kelly escorted Clare into The Emerald Isle with his hand at her waist. As usual he was hailed by some of the regulars, a couple of the waitresses, and the bartender.

"Don't tell me. Let me guess," chided Clare. "You've been here before."

Smiling down at her, he said, "A couple of times." Turning his head toward the bartender, he asked, "Is there any room at the table, Paddy?"

"You got it all to yourself, Kelly," replied the bartender as he vigorously wiped a glass. "It's a bit early for Michael, as you know. Your mother has her ways of insisting he eats his dinner on time."

"Mother" came out sounding more like "mither" in the man's strong Irish accent, but his smile was universal. Clare couldn't help but smile back at the bartender's contagious good humor. Usually she didn't care for bars but this one was different. Even with the clinking of glasses, the laughter, and people chatting, it was possible to talk without having to shout at the person across the table, and the lighting was adequate enough to walk around without bumping into tables and other patrons.

Kelly's hand guided her farther into the pub until they reached a large, round table in the back. He pulled out a chair and invited her to sit down, taking the chair next to her for himself.

Fiona came to the table almost immediately. "So what'll it be, Kelly?"

"I'll have the usual, Fiona." Shifting his glance to Clare, he asked, "What would you like, Lily?"

"I'd like a glass of white wine, please."

"And bring menus, Fiona. I'm starving."

"So what's new?" the waitress drawled. "Kevin came limping in about an hour ago and ordered three cheeseburgers and fries. Then he was going home for supper. He probably ate all of that too. Don't you McGinnises ever get filled up?"

Kelly laughed. "Kevin's wife fixes liver and onions once a week. He hates liver and onions so he fortifies himself before he goes home on the nights he's expecting it."

Fiona went away chuckling and shaking her head.

During the next hour, they ate a leisurely meal and sipped their drinks, sometimes making conversation, sometimes content just to sit in silence. Clare soaked up the atmosphere and Kelly soaked up being with Clare.

One of the other patrons, a burly man with a hearty smile, challenged Kelly to a dart game. There was a spirited exchange between the two men, an apparently running debate concerning other games between the two. Kelly declined the challenge but Clare encouraged him to go ahead.

Kelly hesitated. "Why don't you play with us? I don't want to leave you alone at the table."

"I've never played darts before. You don't need an amateur. I'd rather watch you play." When he still hesitated, she added, "Go on, Kelly. Please. I would like to see how the game is played."

"All right," he conceded. "I'll only play one game."

One game turned into two and then they played a third and a fourth game. It took awhile for Clare to understand the scoring system, since they started with a score and deducted the amount of the total of each throw instead of starting at zero and adding until the one with the highest score won. They started with five hundred and one and subtracted the total of the numbers thrown by three darts, ending by having to hit a double in order to go out and then win the game.

She had always thought the game was simply to throw the dart and hit a number, with luck. Once she understood how the game was played, Clare saw how good Kelly was. He hit the number he was aiming for most of the time, which proved he had plenty of experience. It was also clear that his opponent was no slouch either.

A deep male voice spoke her thoughts aloud. "He always hits what he aims for, that lad." She heard a rumbling chuckle and then the voice added, "And not just in darts."

Clare turned her head in the direction of the voice and saw she was no longer sitting alone at the table. A large hand was extended across the table and she found herself clasping the rough paw of Michael McGinnis. Before he introduced himself, Clare already knew who the older man was. He had the same dark hair and blue eyes, but most of all he had a look of devilment in his eyes she had seen before—a number of times. Kelly's father was of stockier build than his son with a thick crop of gray and white hair. He was dressed for a chilly night instead of a warm pub, wearing a bulky white Irish sweater under a tweed sport coat.

In his forthright Irish way, he charged ahead. "Well, Clare Denham. It's a pleasure to finally meet you."

Her eyes went wide in surprise. "How do you know who I am?"

"Well, now. I could say I have the second sight, but the truth is Kelly came in here all in a dither last weekend because he couldn't find one Clare Denham. You're sitting here at the McGinnis table and Kelly McGinnis is just over there. That makes you Clare Denham." Leaning back in his chair, he accepted the glass of dark brown beer from the ever-efficient Fiona. "Tell me, Miss Denham, do you like children?"

Clare gave a choked laugh of surprise at the abrupt

change of subject. "Yes, I like children. Why do you ask?"

"It's important to love children. Not every woman does, you know." Again, he changed directions as rapidly as a rabbit being chased by a fox. "I see Kelly finally found you." His chuckle was one of pure enjoyment. "Poor lad. He was at his wits' end but it did him good. A prize is not valued if it's won too easily."

Clare was floundering like a boat that had broken away from its moorings, feeling way out of her depth and unable to swim in the turbulent currents of his conversation.

Luckily the dart game finished and Kelly came back to the table. "Hi, Pop. I hope you introduced yourself to Clare." As he took the chair next to Clare's, he slanted a quick look at her face and saw her slightly stunned expression. Sitting back, he put his arm across the back of her chair. "Have you been giving Clare a bad time, Pop?"

"Not at all. Not at all. We've been getting acquainted is all. How did you fare with Shamus, Kel?"

"We broke even. I won four and he won four."

To Clare, Kelly's father explained, "Shamus and Kelly have a long-standing feud with the dartboard."

"I thought the purpose was to try to beat your opponent, not the board."

"There are no hard feelings on either side if the board beats you or if you beat the board. Much friendlier that way, wouldn't you say."

"I never thought of it that way. I thought the whole idea of any game was the competition between opponents. Someone wins and someone loses."

Kelly's father made a sound that sounded like a cat being strangled. "That is how wars are fought," he said disgustedly. "It isn't the way to make and keep friends. To compete with the game itself is much better than to compete with people. It should be the same between a man and a woman. Them against the world. It's the only way. Not against each other."

Kelly smiled over at Clare. "My father believes in the old saying, 'Make love, not war.' "

"And a good saying it is," proclaimed his father. "More people should believe in it as well." Looking at someone behind Kelly, he asked. "Isn't that right, Fiona?"

"Sure it is, Michael McGinnis," replied the waitress as she came around the table to place another pint of beer in front of him. "I haven't the faintest idea what you're talking about but I'll agree with whatever you say." To Kelly, she asked, "Would you care for another drink?"

"No thanks, Fiona." Kelly pushed back his chair. "We have to go, Pop. Don't forget about tomorrow."

"We'll be there, me boy," stated Michael with a wink and a nod. Getting to his feet, he extended his hand again to Clare. "It's been a pleasure, Clare Denham."

"It's been—interesting, Mr. McGinnis."

"That it has, my girl. I'll be seeing—"

"We have to be going, Pop," Kelly said quickly, drawing Clare away with him before his father finished his sentence. "See you later."

On their way back to Mrs. Hamilton's house, Kelly stopped at an ice cream parlor and came back with three cartons of different flavors. Sliding behind the wheel, he handed her the bag to hold.

The heavy weight made Clare curious about how much ice cream he had bought. A peek into the bag revealed three one-gallon containers. "Playing darts must really work up an appetite. You don't really plan to eat all this yourself, do you?"

Starting the car, Kelly smiled over at her as she

held the ice cream on her lap. "I thought you might help me eat some of it."

"It depends on what kind you got."

"I got chocolate chip, chocolate ripple, and I got Oreo cookie ice cream for you."

"How do you know I like Oreo cookie ice cream?"

"A man knows these things," he stated smugly.

"Does a man also know that ice cream is very cold and melts?" she asked sweetly as she lifted the bag off her lap briefly.

Taking the hint, he pressed his foot down on the accelerator.

Several times during the following day, Clare found herself smiling at the oddest times as she remembered the previous evening. A couple of her customers looked at her curiously several times, but she didn't even notice. A simple thing like eating ice cream had turned into a sensual experience, as Kelly began to feed her spoonfuls of the different flavors. Then he set out to kiss her after each spoonful to warm her lips after eating the cold ice cream. The combination of the chilled dessert and their warm breath changed a teasing gesture into a totally passionate experience. What they had started in the kitchen had ended up in Clare's bedroom.

As Clare turned into the lane leading to Mrs. Hamilton's house, she almost laughed out loud as she remembered the way Kelly had scooped out the ice cream with a gleam of anticipation in his eyes. He made a big production out of dishing out the ice cream with exaggerated movements like a demented soda jerk, making her laugh.

She marveled how Kelly could make the most everyday activity into an event. He possessed a joy for life she envied and she never knew what he was going to do next.

Coming around the curve, she suddenly had to put on the brakes to prevent bashing into a truck parked in the driveway. She couldn't go around it because a car was parked next to the truck, blocking the drive. She got out of Sadie and walked between the truck and the car, around the other car, past another car. There was another truck and a van parked in front of the house. What in blue blazes was going on? Mrs. Hamilton's driveway had become a parking lot.

It wasn't until she walked around the large van that she saw a familiar vehicle. It was a black Blazer.

Coming around Kelly's truck, she almost tripped over a large metal tool box because she wasn't looking where she was going. What had caught her attention was a man dressed in overalls up on a ladder in front of one of the second-story windows. He happened to turn his head enough so she could see his face.

"Who are you?" she yelled.

Kelly's brother looked down and saw Clare staring up at him. "Hi, Clare. I'm Daniel McGinnis." he replied calmly.

"What are you doing up there?"

"This shutter is loose."

That explanation didn't help one bit. Were all the McGinnises masters of evasion? There was one McGinnis who had better come up with some answers real quick. "Where's Kelly?"

"He should be in your bedroom."

He should be locked up, she muttered to herself as she started up the steps toward the front door.

The minute she opened the front door, she wondered if she had somehow wandered into someone else's house. A drop cloth was on the floor in the doorway to the living room and one side of the door frame had been taken off. There was the sound of an electric saw coming from the living room, and she peeked inside to see a complete stranger bending over a pair of sawhorses while sawing a piece of wood molding. This time she didn't even bother to ask who he was or what he was doing.

There was a muffled sound of hammering and several voices coming from the second floor. The rasping sound of sandpaper against wood drew her eyes to the stairs where Kevin was sitting halfway up the stairs sanding one of the new railings that had been installed. His cast-covered foot was resting on the step below him. He looked up and grinned while she stared at him. She gave him a forced smile in return. Then she heard more sounds of activity upstairs and a woman's voice coming from the dining room. Another woman's laughter drew Clare in that direction. Megan was placing a stack of dishes on the dining room table, which was liberally covered with numerous plates and bowls of food covered with foil and plastic wrap. It looked like there was enough food for an army.

"Megan?"

Looking up, Megan smiled. "Hi, Clare." Reaching for a carrot stick, she dipped it into a small bowl. "Here, try this. My sister-in-law Moira made this dip. It's terrific."

Feeling as though she was sleepwalking, Clare moved toward the table and ignored the carrot stick Megan held out to her. "Megan," she said slowly as though Megan had difficulty understanding the English language. "What is going on here?"

Since Clare didn't seem to want the carrot, Megan bit off a chunk and calmly chewed, her eyes scrunching up with supreme ecstasy. "You really should taste this dip, Clare. Moira will give you the recipe if you want it. She made it up herself."

Clare's patience, never her strongest virtue, was as thin as a cheating husband's excuses. "Megan, if someone doesn't tell me what is going on here in the next ten seconds, I'm going to make an Irish temper look like a calm sea breeze. This happens to be my house and there are people all over the place with hammers and saws. I think I have a right to know what is going on."

Accustomed to heated words, although not from Clare, Megan answered calmly, "Kelly mentioned you needed to fix up the house in order to sell it, so those of us who could came to do what we could to help. I gave myself a day off so I could come too. I didn't want to miss this. Plus I admit I wanted to see this house." She raised her hand. "I know. I'm a snoop. So true. So true."

"But why would your family go to so much trouble for someone they hardly know?"

"Because Kelly asked us."

It was such a simple statement but apparently said it all.

Megan opened her mouth to say something more but the abrupt clanging of a dinner bell stopped her. Several women came through the door between the kitchen and the dining room carrying more platters of food. Saws were shut off, doors opened and closed, and the sound of heavy boots on the stairs and the wooden floors replaced the sound of the turned-off saws.

Suddenly Clare found herself surrounded by a crowd of people. Some faces she remembered seeing at the hospital the night Patrick McGinnis was born, and some she had never seen before. Everyone chatted as they filled their plates with the food several of the women had uncovered. Kelly's mother shoved a plate into Clare's hands and insisted she eat something, piling food on Clare's plate when she didn't do it herself.

Clare mumbled a thank-you in a dazed voice.

She looked around but couldn't find Kelly in the crowd.

There wasn't enough room for everyone to sit down at the table, so people found chairs, sat on the stairs or in the kitchen nook, or wandered outside to sit on the front steps. There was a lot of laughing, joking, and trading tidbits about the particular work being done. Michael McGinnis came up behind Clare as she stood rooted to the floor, patted her on the shoulder, gave her a cheerful grin, and took his plate of food on into the kitchen. Clare heard him tell one of the men there was beer, and the other man followed Kelly's father into the kitchen.

Maybe that's where Kelly was, thought Clare. Maybe he was getting something to drink. He obviously wasn't getting in line to get anything to eat. He had to be around here someplace and she was going to find him. He had a few million questions to answer.

She tried several times to put down her plate in order to go look for Kelly but someone always kept picking it up and putting it back into her hand with the words, "Eat. Eat."

She mentally threw up her hands and gave up. She went into the kitchen and thanked Kelly's mother and the other Mrs. McGinnises and assorted relations for all the food they had prepared.

Kelly's mother shushed her. "Think nothing of it, me darlin'. The minute Kelly told us of your troubles, we were only too happy to be able to help."

Her troubles? What troubles? "Well, I appreciate everything you all have done. Ah, you wouldn't happen to know where Kelly is, do you? There's something I need to talk to him about."

"I believe he's upstairs somewhere, dear. If you find him, tell him to stop working for a moment so he can get something to eat. The work can wait a few minutes."

"I'll be sure to tell him, Mrs. McGinnis." Among other things, she promised herself.

It would help if she could find him. Occasionally munching on a bite of food from her plate, she looked in every room downstairs with no sign of Kelly. She found Kevin, Daniel, and Michael McGinnis but no Kelly McGinnis. She smiled and chatted and thanked them for coming even though she didn't understand why Kelly had involved his whole family in repairing her house. She was going to find out though. If she ever found the blasted man.

Stepping around the people seated on the stairs, she made her way to her room. The door was open but it took only a brief glance to see he wasn't there. Nor was he in her bathroom. She was determined to find him so she started searching each bedroom. She went from room to room, feeling more and more frustrated as she found only empty rooms.

Until the last one.

It was the smallest bedroom, with a single dormer window in the wall and a sloping ceiling along one side. Kelly was sitting on the dusty floor against one wall with his knees drawn up and his arms resting on his knees. Beside him were several large sheets of paper loosely rolled up. He was staring out the window, a preoccupied expression on his face. He was so deep in thought, he didn't realize he was no longer alone.

"Kelly?"

When he turned his head to look at her, she saw a strange expression darkening his eyes. She slowly came further into the room and knelt down on the floor, still holding her plate. Her anger had instantly dissolved the minute she had seen the bleak look enter his eyes. Placing her hand on his knee, she felt an overpowering need to comfort him, to erase the shadows in his eyes. His pain became hers.

The smile he gave her was a poor imitation. "I swore I wouldn't let it happen again but it did."

Softly, she asked, "What happened?"

His mouth twisted as he leaned his head back against the wall, his eyes returning to the view of the blue sky through the small dormer window. His hands clenched into fists and he swore under his breath. "I didn't want to care again. I really didn't want to care for anything or anyone again other than my family."

"Would that be so horrible?" She held her breath, waiting for him to answer and so afraid she wouldn't like his answer.

He brought his gaze back to her face. "The caring isn't horrible. Losing something you care about is."

Was he referring to his ex-wife or the house he had lost or both? "What is it you care about that you don't want to care about?"

He picked up the rolled papers off the floor and handed them to her. "Last night I got out the notes I made when I went through the house to make the estimate. I was going to plan which repairs would get done today and who would do them. Five hours later, I had this to show for my time."

Putting down her plate, Clare unrolled the sheaves of paper. The drawings were sketches of several rooms. Each had the room description underneath, which was just as well because she couldn't recognize the rooms from the drawings. There were a variety of changes in each room over and above the necessary repairs. Some were drastic changes, some were minor, but each greatly improved the appearance of every room. Even to her untrained eye, she could see the skill and creativity in each line . . . and the way he cared about the house.

There was a certain wistfulness in her voice she couldn't disguise. "It would be wonderful if the house could look like this."

"It could."

"No," she stated firmly. "I have to be realistic, Kelly. As much as I would like to see all these marvelous changes made to the house, I can't afford all these renovations, Kelly. You know that. I have to sell the house."

He took the papers from her and rolled them back up. "You could sell the house to me."

Nine

Clare stared at him, unsure whether she had heard him right. "*You* want to buy Mrs. Hamilton's house? But—"

"But why would I want to buy a house after I had ranted and raved about never getting another house? I don't blame you for not believing me. I found it hard to believe myself around three o'clock this morning when I discovered why I wanted to make all these changes." He laid the sketches aside and took her hand in his. "I want this house, Clare. I don't want you to sell it to anyone else but me."

"I—see," she murmured, not really seeing anything at all. She could only take in so many surprises in one day. Finally she said, "I guess your money is as good as anyone else's."

He leaned over and kissed her lightly. "Good. That's settled." Raising his head enough to see her face, he smiled down at her until his eyes went to her mouth, slightly parted and moist. If it wasn't for half his family being in the house, he would gladly accept the invitation of her tempting mouth and body.

No longer smiling, he again touched her lips with his, lingering briefly, all too briefly, over her mouth. Forcing himself away from her, he levered himself up, getting to his feet. "I'd better check on the workers to make sure they're fixing *my* house right."

She heard the possessive tone in his voice. So that's why he had arranged for his family to come to the house. It wasn't to help her at all. It had been for him, not her. She should be relieved to find a buyer for the house so quickly. After all, she would have the money to pay Mrs. Hamilton's medical and living expenses for quite awhile. Selling the house would solve a lot of problems.

She should be happy to have the old house off her hands. So why wasn't she?

Feeling incredibly deflated, she withdrew her hand from his and picked up her plate. "Your mother asked me to tell you to come and eat something." Her face was blank and unsmiling as she stood up. She moved toward the door, her spine stiff with tension.

Puzzled, Kelly stared at her, wondering why she had withdrawn from him so abruptly. He hadn't meant to spring his desire to buy the house on her like that but he wasn't going to take back his words. He *did* want the house. *And* her. His timing may not have been the best in telling her about his plans for the house but now he was relieved to have it out of the way so he could concentrate on her. As he watched her leave the room, he had the feeling that getting her to believe just how involved he wanted to be with her wasn't going to be all that easy. He was going to need all the Irish luck he could find to convince her he was no longer interested in a temporary affair.

Following her down the stairs, he heard the voices of various members of his family. It was obvious he wasn't going to be able to talk to Clare alone for a while. Getting some of his family to help fix up the house had been a good idea several days ago, but now he wished they weren't there. He had wanted to see how Clare related to his family as well as have help getting the house in shape. Now he wanted to be alone with her.

His father was waiting at the bottom of the stairs, cutting off any chance of going after Clare. He wanted to know what Kelly wanted him to do next so Kelly had no choice but to postpone talking to Clare for the moment.

Clare helped clear off the dining room table and joined the other women in the kitchen. At first it was a strain to try to make conversation when all she could think of was what Kelly had told her about buying the house. In a short time, though, she was unable to resist listening to the lively conversations going on around her. Each one had a story or an anecdote to tease one of the others about or to tell about one of the other members. The stories continued after the dishes were all done and put away and the women sat down at the kitchen nook with cups of coffee.

Moira was curious about the salon and asked a few questions concerning the type of beauty treatments available. Megan was the salon's best advertisement and the most enthusiastic, convincing Moira she should go to the salon too.

Occasionally Clare could detect the sound of the repairs continuing in the house, but she stayed in the kitchen. She was enjoying the company, and she had no desire to see what was being done to the house. One of the things she was curious about was whether or not she was supposed to pay for all the repairs being done or if Kelly was planning to absorb the expense since he was planning to buy the house.

Kelly's mother got around to talking about the plans being made for a birthday party to be held Saturday evening for Kelly's father. She brought out a list of who was going to bring what, reminding Megan not to forget to pick up the cake from the bakery. Clare managed to hide her surprise when Mrs. McGinnis automatically included her, stating she had put Clare down to bring three dozen dinner rolls. When Kelly's mother glanced up at Clare for confirmation, Clare gave her a weak smile and nodded.

Now what was she going to do? Mrs. McGinnis was taking it for granted Clare knew all about the birthday party and would be coming with Kelly. She was becoming more and more involved with the McGinnis family whether she wanted to be or not. Unfortunately she wanted to be. She liked being involved with the loving McGinnis family, but not under false pretenses.

By nine o'clock the last member of the McGinnis work force had driven away—except Kelly.

Clare shut the door and leaned wearily against it. She needed time to think about all the things that had happened today, but she knew she wasn't going to have the time she needed. Pushing herself away from the door, she straightened her spine and took a deep, steadying breath. Kelly had walked his parents out to their car and would be back in a few minutes. That was all the time she was going to have to collect her thoughts before he returned.

She went into the living room and sank down onto the sofa, kicking off her shoes before tucking her legs under her. She didn't bother turning on any lights in the room, preferring the light coming from the hallway. She heard the front door open and then shut but she stayed where she was. She was going to take advantage of every second she could get before he found her.

His footsteps went away from the living room and toward the dining room and kitchen instead of into the living room, so she had a moment's reprieve. She tried to use the time to gather her thoughts into some sort of order before he came looking for her.

Before she was ready, he came into the living room carrying a bottle of white wine and two glasses.

"I've been looking for you, Lily. Why are you sitting in the dark?"

"It seemed appropriate. I'm in the dark about a lot of things."

Kelly turned on one of the lamps before sitting down beside her on the sofa. He handed her one of the glasses and poured some wine for her while she held the glass. Then he filled his own. "What are you in the dark about?"

She brought the glass up to her mouth and drank from it. Lowering it, she said, "Well, let's see. I could start with your arranging to have your family come here to do work on this house without consulting me. There's also the news flash that you want to buy this house." Taking another sip from the glass, she added, "It also seems I'm invited to your father's birthday party next Saturday night, which was somewhat of a surprise since I didn't know anything about it."

Settling back against the back of the sofa after placing the wine bottle on the coffee table, he asked, "Is that it?"

"For starters."

"Can I have a sip of this wine first?"

"You can drink the whole bottle as long as I get a few answers eventually."

He proceeded to take a drink, rolling the wine around on his tongue. "Okay. What was the first question again?"

"Why didn't you tell me your family was coming here to work on the house?"

He placed the stem of his wine glass on his thigh. His eyes narrowed as he studied her face. "Do you resent my family being here?"

"I resent your making plans concerning this house without consulting me. I answered your question. You've seen how it's done. Now answer mine."

"It was a way to get the repairs done without costing you money that you don't have. There's still a couple of things left to do but I can finish them. I didn't mention it because you would have objected."

"Of course I would have objected. Your family went to a lot of trouble today. Your mother and sisters and sisters-in-law cooked all the food and left their homes to come here to feed everyone. I hope your brothers didn't take time away from their own work in order to help you."

"Kevin had the day off and Daniel is on vacation. My father is retired. There were a couple of men who work for me who helped out today but they're on my payroll. Since I plan to own the house, the cost of the repairs is on me." He gave her a crooked smile. "The women came mostly out of curiosity. They wanted to see this house—and you."

Her eyes widened in surprise but she remember there were other questions to be answered. "Is your family aware of the fact that you want to buy this house?"

"No."

"Your family came here just because you asked them to? They were willing to spend their time helping someone they don't even know very well?" Her voice rose, clearly finding it hard to believe people would do such a magnanimous favor for someone they had just met.

He raised his glass and drank the rest of the wine. "They know you." Leaning forward, he picked up the wine bottle and filled his glass again. "You find my family hard to understand, don't you?"

She stared down into her glass, swirling the wine around slowly. "I think you are very lucky to have the family you have. I admit I haven't had any experience with a family like yours but that doesn't mean I can't appreciate them." Finishing the wine in her glass, she continued, "Did you know your mother has me down for three dozen dinner rolls to bring to your father's birthday party?"

He chuckled. "No, I didn't know that. It looks like you've been adopted into the family. How do you feel about that?"

"Stunned."

Extending her glass toward him, he took the hint and poured more wine into her glass. "You'll get used to it."

Would she? she wondered pensively. He was implying she would be seeing his family on a regular basis and it wasn't fair. She did like his family but they were his family, not hers. He was putting her in the uncomfortable position of being a fifth wheel. She had never felt she really belonged with her own family all the years she was growing up. She certainly didn't belong with his family. She didn't belong to anyone.

Mrs. Hamilton had given her the means of making a living and had cared for Clare in her own way, but Clare had respected the boundaries of the older woman's friendship and never stepped over them. She wasn't going to step over the boundaries of the McGinnis family territory either.

Uncurling her legs, she took her glass with her as she got off the couch. She went to the window and ran her hand over the walnut wood of the window frame. Remembering the sketch Kelly had made of the living room, she asked, "Do you plan to use the same wood when you change the house?"

Kelly tilted his head as he studied her from the sofa. "I plan to stay with the same wood already in the house. The changes I want to make will be to add to the house, not to take away from it." Watching her carefully, he asked, "You don't like the idea of my buying this house, do you?"

Dropping her hand, she transferred her gaze to the window, looking out at the dark shadows of the trees dimly illuminated by the moon. "The house has to be sold and you want to buy it. Why would I object to that?"

"I don't know. Why do you?"

Turning around to face him, she replied honestly, "I don't. Really I don't. You'll make the house a thing of pure beauty, Kelly. I know that. The house is lucky to be wanted by someone who will take care of it."

"Then why are you drawing away from me?" he asked quietly.

"Am I?" She left the window and went over to stand behind one of the Queen Anne chairs and laid her hand on the back. "I was surprised, that's all. After you told me what had happened to your own house, you were the last person I thought would be interested in this place." Her hand began to stroke the tapestry under her hand. "I hope you want the furniture too. It all belongs with the house."

Kelly leaned forward, his forearms resting on his knees. "I won't buy this house if it's going to come between us, Clare. I would like to own it, I admit that. It's the first house that has caught my imagination in a long time but I don't need it."

"Maybe the house needs you."

He stood up and came over to her, taking her hand and drawing her from around the chair. He took the glass of wine out of her hand and set it down on a nearby table.

"What about you? What do you need?"

Her gaze shifted away from him. "Me? I don't need anything."

If she had been looking at him, she would have seen the look of disappointment cross his face. His hands clamped around her waist and drew her against him. He looked down at her startled eyes as he leaned toward her, his eyes dark and hungry.

Against her mouth, he murmured, "I was hoping you would say you needed me."

The moment his mouth covered her parted lips, she felt a need stronger than her common sense, more compelling than keeping her sanity. A soft sound of pleasure turned into a moan of surrender when his hands moved to her hips to bring her lower body into his aggressive male heat. Her arms snaked around his neck and she arched her body to fit the contours of his, loving the feel of him, loving the taste of him—loving him.

The time for talking was over. The time for loving began. The urgency to settle their differences vanished, to be replaced by the craving to fulfill the promise of supreme satisfaction they knew they would find in each other.

Unable to wait a moment longer to make her his, Kelly stripped away her clothing and then his own. He eased her down onto the sofa and feasted his eyes on her naked body before covering her with his heated flesh. His tongue entered her mouth at the same time as his body joined with hers, claiming her completely.

Kelly found he had to have more than her breathtaking response. "Say it. Say you need me," he ordered, his voice hoarse with restraint.

Her hands clutched his back. "I do," she breathed. "I do need you."

His breath caught as her words flowed over him, satisfying him in a way that reached down deep inside him. He gripped her hands and drew them over her head, threading his fingers through hers as he had done before. She was the lifeline to hold on to as he thrust into her, drowning in her and never wanting to be saved.

"Clare," he murmured against her throat, sliding over her in long, bonding movements. He felt spirals of pleasure along his spine signaling the culmination of his release, but he didn't want the lovemaking to end yet. His fingers tightened fiercely around hers as he reached for the pot of gold at the end of the rainbow—and found it. Shimmering lights and treasure beyond his wildest dreams flowed through him and he gasped her name.

It seemed forever for Clare to float back to earth. Then she felt as though she was floating again as Kelly picked her up in his arms and carried her up the stairs to her bedroom.

When Clare woke up the following morning, she was alone.

Going through the usual routine of showering, dressing, and putting on her makeup, she tried to banish the depression settling heavily over her. When she went down the stairs, her footsteps slowed as she looked around at the empty hallway below. She felt she was saying good-bye to the house, even though it didn't officially belong to Kelly yet. Already it seemed to be more his house than hers. Her hand smoothed over the banister as she continued down the stairs, her gaze going over the repaired rails.

The changes wrought the day before were minor but obvious. Windows had been replaced, the areas of dry rot had been repaired, and the house stood silent and sturdy around her.

Nothing had really been settled last night except that Kelly was going to buy the house. The passion between them was as strong and undeniable as ever.

There had been nothing said about tomorrow or the next day. They had concentrated on the moment and each other during the night but the night was over. This was today and she wasn't sure about tomorrow.

In the afternoon, Clare received a call from her realtor. Kelly had contacted him early that morning about wanting to buy the house. He apparently didn't believe in wasting any time. The realtor reminded her there was a contract to be signed and agreements to reach concerning the contents of the house. His advice was to charge extra for the furnishings but Clare instructed him to draw up the contract to include the furniture in the price she was asking for the house. The realtor tried to talk her out of it but she remained firm. Since the new owner would have to honor the leases for the greenhouses and the garden plots, it seemed to Clare only fair for the contract to also include all the drapes and furniture.

A little later, after she hung up the phone, she realized she would have to find someplace else to live. The thought of a small apartment or a condominium didn't really appeal to her after living in the gracious old house but she had to live somewhere. She had told the realtor that the new owner could move into the house in thirty days so she had a little time to look for someplace to move her few belongings.

Every time the phone rang, she half expected the caller to be Kelly but the day passed without hearing from him. She did hear indirectly from one of the members of the McGinnis family though. When she consulted the appointment book to see what her schedule would be for Thursday, she saw the name Moira McGinnis listed for a facial. Kelly's sister-in-law had asked for her.

She decided to stay at the salon until it closed at ten even though her last appointment had been at four-thirty. The thought of going back to that big empty house filled her with dread and she was going to put it off as long as she could. She put her time to good use by taking an inventory of the numerous tubes of lipstick and eye shadow, a tedious and time-consuming job that needed to be done and one that everyone kept putting off.

At seven o'clock, Kelly finally did call.

"What are you still doing at work? Denise said you were off at five. I've been waiting for you."

"I didn't know you were waiting for me."

"When are you coming home? Our dinner is getting cold."

Home? Dinner? Clare held the phone away from her and looked at it as if looking at it would make sense out of the words coming through it. It didn't help. Raising the phone back, she asked, "Have I missed something somewhere? How am I supposed to know you're waiting for me if you don't tell me? Did it ever occur to you to talk to me instead of Denise?"

"You have a habit of asking multiple questions. I phoned the salon but you were busy and I didn't have time to wait until you were free. So when are you coming home?"

He used that word so easily. Home. He thought of the house in a way she hadn't allowed herself to feel.

"I'll be there in about twenty minutes," she promised with a decided lack of enthusiasm.

The rest of the week followed the pattern set from that night. When she left the salon, she drove to Mrs. Hamilton's house where either she fixed dinner or Kelly brought something from a fast food restaurant. She signed the contract for the house on her day off but it wasn't mentioned between them that night, although the realtor had told her he was expecting Kelly to come in to his office to sign the papers later that afternoon.

It was as though they were in a holding pattern like two planes flying in tandem but not too sure where they would land.

Kelly never stayed an entire night with her. Sometime after she had fallen asleep, he would dress and return to his cold lifeless condo. He hated leaving her but he couldn't stay.

Clare hated to wake up alone but she never asked him to stay.

On Friday evening, Clare decided she should go shopping for groceries and Kelly agreed to come with her. The simple everyday task of pushing a shopping cart up and down the aisles of a grocery became a challenge to prevent Kelly from buying out the store. He completely ignored her list and chose whatever took his fancy, usually grabbing two of everything he wanted. He kept putting items into the cart and she tried to take out what she didn't need.

Several times Clare was stopped by women customers who were regular patrons of the salon. They chatted briefly with Clare before moving on.

After the third woman went on to finish her shopping, Kelly stated, "You have a number of satisfied customers."

"I'd like to think so."

Picking up a box of dried apricots, he read the label and then asked, "Why did you choose cosmetology?"

She took the box out of his hand and set it back on the shelf. "We don't need dried apricots."

"I'll concede the apricots if you'll answer my question. Why cosmetology?"

"When I was in school I tried out for every play put on by the English class but I couldn't act my way out of a wet paper bag. I still hung around the stage to watch the ones who could act, and a sympathetic teacher decided to show me how to put makeup on the players. I discovered I was very good at it and like creating different expressions, different ages. When my parents insisted I go to law school, I rebelled and left home. Mrs. Hamilton gave me a job in one of her stores and later lent me the money to get my degree in cosmetology."

Kelly thought about what she had told him as they continued down the aisle. His parents had been so supportive of his decision to go into business for himself, even though there would have been easier ways to make a living. No wonder she was so loyal to Mrs. Hamilton. The older woman let Clare be what she wanted to be, helping her to achieve her goals instead of holding her back.

He didn't want to hold her back from being what she wanted to be but he did want to be part of who she was.

Several times Kelly came close to telling Clare how he felt about her, especially when he held her in his arms after they had made love, but a niggling doubt gnawed at him. He hadn't paid much attention to how his ex-wife had related to his family before they were married, taking it for granted she got along well with them. Everyone else did. It was only after they were married that she had balked at spending so much time with them. After his divorce, Megan had bluntly informed him that his ex-wife had rarely joined in, or even tried to. He hadn't known that then. This time he was going to know before, not after.

He had to be certain Clare could accept the close involvement he had with his family. By the end of the week, he decided it was time to find out. They couldn't keep going on this way. They were in limbo and he hated it.

The occasion he chose was his father's birthday party where all the members of his family would be on hand. His parents still lived in the large house where he had grown up. There was plenty of room for putting babies down for naps, for touch football games on the back lawn, for groups to gather to chat or play cards.

The minute they arrived, Clare was whisked off to the kitchen by one of the women, taking her contribution of food with her. Mrs. McGinnis greeted her with a hug and set her to work along with some of the other women. Some of the older children were helping out too and Clare greeted Maire and several of her cousins, promising to let them beat her at gin rummy later. She peeled carrots for the relish tray and chatted with Megan and several other of the women who had also been assigned their own jobs to do.

Kelly had gone outside where his father was holding court at the barbecue pit. Taking a beer out of the tub of iced drinks, he joined the other men who were grouped around the pit while keeping an eye on some of the children who were playing around them. Several times, Kelly found excuses to go into the kitchen to see Clare, enduring the teasing from the womenfolk with good grace. To his mother's delight, Clare gave as good as she got when she came into some of the teasing along with Kelly.

Along with Kelly's odd possessive behavior, Clare was puzzled by several strange references to an upcoming wedding with expectant glances in her direction, as if she was supposed to make some kind of comment. Whenever she looked up during the day, she found Kelly watching her intently. The nephews and nieces all called her Aunt Clare but she considered the title an honorary one and didn't think much about it.

Later, after everyone had eaten their fill of the abundance of food, a large birthday cake disappeared almost as soon as Kelly's father had blown out the candles. Michael made a little speech thanking everyone for coming and for all the presents he received. Looking at Clare and Kelly who were standing together along with the rest of the family clustered around him, he grinned and winked, saying some presents were priceless. The older man had tears in his eyes as he thanked Kelly for indeed making this a special day.

Clare looked from Kelly to his father back to Kelly again, wondering what Mr. McGinnis was talking about. She had seen the fishing rod and fishing tackle Kelly had given his father. She supposed the fishing equipment was of good quality but certainly nothing to get emotional about, unless Kelly's father considered fishing a moving experience.

As the day wore on, there were several other incidents which left Clare with the feeling that everyone knew something about her and Kelly that she wasn't aware of, or that they were under a misconception of what their relationship was.

Later Clare couldn't remember what she had replied when members of Kelly's family offered her congratulations. Hopefully she hadn't sounded as stupid as she felt. For some reason, Kelly's family took it for granted that Clare was going to be a permanent fixture. Whether it was something Kelly had said to them or whether they were only guessing, she was determined to talk to Kelly to get him to clear up the misunderstanding.

She didn't get a chance to talk to him privately until they were driving back to the house.

He gave her the opening she wanted when he asked if she had enjoyed herself. "Yes," she replied. "Of course I did." Then she brought up the subject that had been bothering her. "Kelly, I've heard some odd comments all day concerning you and me. Your family seems to be under the wrong impression about our relationship."

"They know exactly what our relationship is. I told them."

She stared at him. "You told them we were having an affair?"

He calmly watched the road as he stated, "I told my parents there was a possibility we would be getting married if everything worked out today."

He might have been discussing the weather. She felt anything but nonchalant. "What do you mean, if everything worked out today?"

"Wait until we get home and then we'll talk about it."

She'd waited long enough. "I think we should talk about it now. What was supposed to happen today for you to decide whether we would get married or not? And, by the way, I have something to say about that ever happening. I want to know, Kelly." She swallowed with difficulty before she continued. "Was today some sort of test I either passed or didn't pass?"

Sighing heavily, Kelly glanced at her quickly before bringing his attention back to the road. "Clare, I had to be sure you would fit in with my family. They are very important to me and I like to spend time with them. If you felt out of place or didn't like to be with them, then we would continue as we have. If I felt you accepted my family, then we would have a chance for a strong marriage."

Clare felt as though she had been hit in the stomach. The simple act of breathing was something she had to concentrate on while her mind whirled with the impact of his words. The day with his family had been a cold-blooded test. He wanted to see how she would interact with his family and then if she passed the test, he would marry her. The arrogance of the man stunned her.

"So," she said in a brittle voice. "Did I pass?"

He drove up the lane toward the house and parked in front. After staring ahead for a few minutes, he turned his head to look at her. "You passed."

"Thank you very much." With clenched fists, she gripped her purse and grabbed for the door handle. "I took a test to get a driver's license but I'll be damned if I take a test in order to get a marriage license. Damn you, Kelly McGinnis. How dare you submit me to a test to see if I qualify to become your wife?"

His hand reached out to stop her from leaving his car. "Just listen to me a moment before you fly off the handle. My ex-wife couldn't adjust to the close ties I have with my family. I wasn't going to get myself into that no-win situation again."

Jerking away from him, she opened the door. "I don't come with a guarantee, Kelly." Springing out of the car, she snapped, "Try a washing machine. *That* comes with a guarantee."

Kelly didn't go after her. Slamming his hand against the steering wheel, he watched her as she ran up the steps and disappeared through the door.

His motives had made sense to him originally but now he could see how she saw his actions. The day had come off like an audition for a part in his life. What an idiot he was. A real smooth operator. It was going to take every ounce of Irish luck to get her to listen to him.

Ten

Clare spent the following two days on an emotional seesaw, hoping she would never see Kelly McGinnis again and wondering why he hadn't come after her. She was furious with him, red-hot furious with him— and loved him more than her life.

She went through the daylight hours trying to pretend everything was normal. But the nights were anything but normal. They were long and lonely with too many hours to fill, too many hours to listen for the phone to ring, too many hours to wait for dawn to arrive while she restlessly wandered around the house, unable to sleep in the bed where she had shared passionate hours with Kelly. The sofa was off-limits for the same reason.

She couldn't believe their relationship was going to end like this. She couldn't be that wrong about the strength of the feelings between them. Even though they had parted with angry words, she had to believe they could work things out. She had to keep believing that.

By Tuesday it was a struggle to carry on without

letting the depression deep inside her overwhelm her. She managed to smile and chat with the various clients in the salon and went about her work as if her world hadn't come apart at the seams.

By five o'clock she was worn out with the strain of trying to keep up a front of normality. She went into her office and shut the door, putting off the drive to the large lonely house in the country. Sinking down in her chair, she debated going out to eat somewhere to put off the time she had to return to the house. Unfortunately she didn't think she could eat a bite.

There was a knock on her door and she said unenthusiastically, "Come in."

When the door opened, she looked up, expecting to see one of her employees. She blinked several times as though her eyes were playing tricks on her. Staring at the small figure standing in the doorway, Clare wondered if she was seeing things or if her lack of sleep was catching up to her.

A small boy dressed as a leprechaun stood in the doorway holding something green and leafy in his hand. He came forward and held out the bunch of greenery toward her. When he was closer to her, Clare recognized him. He was Sean McGinnis, Kelly's nephew.

She accepted the green bouquet and discovered upon closer examination that the bouquet was shamrocks. Actually they were three-leaf clovers instead of four-leaf clovers but Clare wasn't about to quibble. She knew what the clovers were meant to represent. Her heart thudded loudly in her chest, hope beginning to stir where despair had previously taken hold.

"Hello, Sean."

The little boy apparently had his instructions and conversation with Auntie Clare was not part of his orders. He whirled around and left her office. By the time she got out of her chair and came around her desk to follow him, he was out in the mall where his mother was waiting for him.

Clare arrived at the entrance of the salon too late to see Molly and Sean turn into the ice cream parlor to get Sean's reward for doing what Uncle Kelly had asked him to do.

Still holding the bouquet of shamrocks in her hand, she returned to her office, unaware of the startled looks from the other women in the shop. Miss Denham was acting very peculiar chasing after a little boy dressed like a leprechaun and carrying around a handful of greenery. Very odd.

Clare felt very odd. She sank down into her chair and looked at the wilting bouquet in her hand. What did the visit from Kelly's nephew mean? She wanted to read the gesture as a sign from Kelly that he was thinking of her. That the luck of the Irish was still in force.

Her heart a little lighter, Clare left the salon to drive home. She half expected a black Blazer to be parked in front of the house but the driveway was empty. During the long evening, the phone remained silent. Maybe the shamrocks and the little leprechaun didn't mean what she thought they had meant.

The following day was her day off and she went ahead with her plans. She took special care with her appearance before visiting Mrs. Hamilton. Instead of going to Maddie to borrow some clothes, she chose a white dress in a simple style from her own closet, adding several gold chains and earrings. Her freshly washed hair was arranged carefully in a sophisticated twist, every hair in place the way Mrs. Hamilton preferred her to look.

Yesterday she had called the limousine service to arrange for the trip to the nursing home when she discovered Mrs. Hamilton would be sitting by her window as usual waiting for her. When Clare had phoned the nursing home yesterday, the nurse had told her that Mrs. Hamilton was feeling better and looking forward to seeing her today.

The limousine delivered her to the door of the nursing home and she got out. She stopped to talk to several of the residents who were sitting outside enjoying the beautiful day. Then she went inside to see Mrs. Hamilton.

Mrs. Hamilton's room was the size of a hotel suite, furnished with some of her favorite pieces of furniture brought from the house. It was the largest room in the nursing home and the most expensive. The Queen Anne love seat, chairs, and mahogany tables seemed out of place against the backdrop of white sterile walls and utilitarian hospital bed. Several paintings adorned the walls and a vase of flowers attempted to cheer the room up and make it a little less like a typical nursing-home room.

Usually Mrs. Hamilton was impatiently waiting for her, but today she already had a visitor.

Kelly was sitting next to Mrs. Hamilton, near the window which overlooked the front of the nursing home. There was a tray of coffee on a small table between them. Mrs. Hamilton saw her in the doorway and beckoned her to come in.

"Clare, you're just in time to have coffee with us. I believe you know this gentleman."

Moving toward them, Clare said quietly, "Hello, Kelly."

It seemed longer than two days since he had seen her and he allowed himself the luxury of looking at her for a few seconds. He had planned to be gone by the time Clare arrived but he and Mrs. Hamilton had had quite a lot to talk about. It wasn't easy to remain in his chair when he was aching to take her in his arms but Kelly forced himself to greet her casually. "Hello, Clare." He got up and offered her his chair. Then he spoke to Mrs. Hamilton. "I've taken up enough of your time, Mrs. Hamilton. I'll leave so you two can visit."

Extending her hand, Mrs. Hamilton smiled as she said, "I'm very pleased to meet you, Mr. McGinnis. You've put my mind at ease and I thank you for that."

He took her hand briefly, smiling down at her. "You've helped me too, Mrs. Hamilton. I'd like to come back to see you again."

"I'd like that."

His gaze shifted to Clare who was watching him. A corner of his mouth curved up slightly. And then he turned away and left.

Stunned, Clare stared at the door he had shut behind him.

Mrs. Hamilton was watching her closely. "You didn't know he was coming, did you?"

"No, I didn't."

"I quite enjoyed his visit." She patted her hair carefully and adjusted the collar of her velvet robe. "I do hope he comes to see me again."

There was nothing like an attractive man to bring out the best in any woman of any age. Even as ill as she was, the older woman's cheeks had a spot of color for a change and her eyes were unusually lively. Whatever reason Kelly had for coming to visit Mrs. Hamilton, he had definitely cheered her up.

Mrs. Hamilton began talking about the hairdresser who came to the nursing home, complaining about how inept she was. Clare was relieved to let Mrs. Hamilton keep the conversational ball rolling because for the life of her, Clare couldn't think of much to say. Once the shock of seeing Kelly in Mrs. Hamilton's room wore off, her mind searched for a reason Kelly would visit the older woman. She didn't see him for three days, he sent his nephew to the salon with shamrocks, and then he appeared at the nursing home. Then he left without saying anything to her other than hello. Why?

After an hour, it was apparent Mrs. Hamilton was tiring. "I should be going, Mrs. Hamilton."

The older woman nodded, sorry to see Clare leave but too weary to protest. It had been a very full day. Looking at her watch, she said, "Thank you for coming. I'm sure you have important things to do today so you run along."

"I'll be back next Wednesday unless you need me before then. I'll see if I can get someone else to come to do your hair during the week."

"I would appreciate that, dear." Stating the credo she had lived by during her years of running a business dealing in beauty preparations, she added, "I do feel better when I feel I look nice."

"I'll see what I can arrange," promised Clare before she left the room.

Stopping at the office, she paid Mrs. Hamilton's account to keep it up to date. The cost of the nursing home was prohibitive but necessary for the older woman's care and peace of mind.

After handing over a check, Clare started toward the front door. The depression that usually settled over her every time she came to the nursing home was intensified by the surprise visit from Kelly. He had left without speaking to her other than to say hello and she was at a loss to know why he had come to see Mrs. Hamilton in the first place.

Pushing open the front door, she looked down at the pavement and didn't notice the commotion in front of her until she heard the unusual sound of a horse neighing. Raising her head, she stopped walking and stared openmouthed at the scene in front of her. The elderly people who had been sitting outside had all moved for a closer look at the rare spectacle in front of them, laughing and chatting among themselves.

A chestnut horse hitched to a black buggy was switching his tail, completely oblivious to the sensation he was causing.

Clare walked slowly forward. A man dressed in top hat and tails stood beside the buggy, his eyes finding her in the crowd. He was Kelly's dart-playing opponent, Shamus.

When she stopped several feet away, he swept off his hat and bowed. "Your chariot awaits, my lady."

"I—ah, I have a car waiting."

"I believe the limousine has been sent away, miss." He lifted his hand to indicate she should come with him. "Mr. McGinnis would like the pleasure of your company."

Bemused, Clare took his outstretched hand and let him help her into the buggy. On the seat was a single yellow rose with a drop of dew on a dainty petal. She picked it up and held it up to smell the fragrance. Going around the back of the buggy, the man mounted the steps and sat on the seat ahead of her. He made a clicking noise with his tongue, slapped the reins on the hind quarters of the horse, and left the nursing home behind.

Sitting at her window, Mrs. Hamilton watched the buggy drive away, a smile of delight lighting up her face.

Clare would have enjoyed the ride under different circumstances but she was too occupied with the meaning behind Shamus's words. Mr. McGinnis wanted the pleasure of her company. The startled looks from the people in cars and on the streets went unheeded as Shamus calmly maneuvered the horse and buggy through traffic.

Shamus didn't speak at all during the ride out of town. His attention was on getting them to their destination safely. A horse and buggy wasn't easy to manage compared to a car.

There destination was a lovely green meadow with a grove of trees on three sides. The driver pulled on the reins and stopped the horse before getting out of the buggy to come around to help Clare down. He tied the reins to a branch of one of the trees and then turned to offer her his arm.

The sun beat down on them but a cooling breeze kept the air pleasant as they walked over the coarse thick grass. There was no other sound except nature's cadence: the rustle of leaves and the occasional call from a bird. She was led to the grove of trees where Shamus dropped her arm. When she looked up at him, her eyes were puzzled.

"If you will kindly go through those trees, Miss."

She hesitated, looking at him for a clue to whatever was going on, but his blank expression gave nothing away. Turning toward the trees, she took several steps and then looked back. Shamus was gone. She was alone.

Shrugging, she stepped carefully around a clump of tall grass and made her way through the trees. Looking ahead, a spot of white seemed out of place among the green and brown coloring of the woods and she headed toward it. She raised her hand to brush a branch out of her way as she weaved around the trees and shrubbery, using the bit of white color as her guide.

She slowed her steps when the trees thinned out and she was able to see what was ahead. There was a table in the middle of a small clearing, covered with a white tablecloth set with candles, fine china, and crystal. Standing with his hand on the back of one of the chairs, a man dressed in a tuxedo was waiting for her.

Kelly.

Slowly she came forward. "I don't know what to say."

"How about hello, Kelly."

"Hello, Kelly." Gesturing with her hand at the table, she asked, "Why all this?" she asked quietly.

He came to meet her. "I decided to slow our pace down so we can take time to talk, really talk without interruptions. Things have moved along rather quickly between us and there have been some misunderstandings. I want to clear them up."

Approaching the table, she let her fingers trail over the fine linen of the tablecloth. "You've gone to a lot of trouble. Shamrocks, leprechauns, horse and buggy. Now all this." Her eyes took in the bottle resting in a silver bucket filled with ice. "Champagne?"

"I'm hoping we will have something to celebrate later."

She raised her eyes to meet his. "It wasn't necessary to arrange all this, Kelly. I would have met you anywhere. I want to get everything straightened out too."

He brought his hands up to her shoulders. "We're going to do this right. I've made my quota of mistakes with you and I'm not about to make any more."

She smiled faintly. "In the best lace-curtain Irish tradition?"

"I haven't given you much in the way of romantic gestures since I've known you. I figure you were due a little special attention. It's taken me a couple of days to clear up a few things concerning my work, which is why I sent Sean to the salon so you'd know I was thinking about you."

Clare asked, "Could I ask you something?"

"Anything."

"Why were you visiting Mrs. Hamilton?"

His thumbs moved gently over the soft material of her dress. "The other night I realized I had been so concerned about how you fit into my life, I hadn't looked into how I would fit into yours. I thought it was time I met Mrs. Hamilton. She's an important part of your life, as my family is an important part of mine. I expected you to be involved in my life without my becoming involved in yours."

She moved away from him by taking a step back and several steps away. "I didn't like being tested, Kelly. I prefer to be trusted."

"I know. I was wrong. I never meant to hurt you." He sighed heavily and ran his hand through his hair. "I was so hung up on not making the same mistake twice, I nearly made the biggest mistake of my life."

"There's nothing wrong with making mistakes. We all do. The important thing is to learn from them."

"Oh, I have, Lily. I've leaned a lot of things. One of the things I've learned is not to judge one person by the actions of another. I let my ex-wife poison me against trusting another woman. In the beginning she appeared to like being involved with my family. Later I realized it had all been an act. She resented the way I'm close to the members of my family. I had to be sure you didn't resent my family too." He came over to her and took her arm to turn her around to face him. "They're very important to me, Clare, but so are you. It doesn't even matter to me if you don't care for them. I—"

"I do like your family, Kelly," interrupted Clare. "What I don't like is finding out you've been playing me against them. You include me in your plans only after you've made them, like the day I came home to find your family working on the house. Then you tell me you want to buy the house." Her voice carried a thread of frustrated anger. "You are just full of surprises."

"I want the house so we can live in it together. You deserve that lovely old house as a home and I want to see that you have it."

She was stunned. "You want to live with me in Mrs. Hamilton's house?"

"No. I want you to live with me in *our* house. How do you feel about becoming a full-fledged member of the McGinnis family?"

He was going to have to learn to be more specific. "Are you planning on adopting me?"

Kelly felt his own anger flare until he saw the glint in her eyes, the same expression he had seen before when she was trying to take him down a peg or two. His anger faded. His hands moved to her waist to bring her closer. "No, darling. I want to marry you."

"Why?"

His smile was off center. "You're not going to make this easy for me, are you?"

"No. I don't think I am," she said softly.

His smile grew into a tender expression of amusement. "We'll, I guess you deserve all the words after what I've put you through. I'll start with three words. I love you. I'm a bungling fool but I do love you. I don't want to have to become an old Irishman without you beside me. You don't even have to learn how to dance an Irish jig but I would like you to walk down the aisle with me in front of my family and the whole world."

Clare felt as though she was melting into a puddle of happiness. "When you get around to the words, you do very well."

Kelly's eyes looked oddly vulnerable. "I wouldn't mind hearing a few words myself, Lily."

She raised her hands to cup his face. "I love you,

Kelly. I can't think of anything I would like more than to be your wife and the mother of your children."

His arms tightened around her. "How many?"

Her gaze was on his mouth which was only a few inches from hers. "How many what?"

"Children." His lips touched hers briefly. "How many children are we going to have?"

Her tongue slipped out to trace the taste of him on her mouth. "It's negotiable."

His eyes darkened at the sight of her pink tongue darting out across her lower lip. "We'll discuss it sometime."

She smiled up at him. "Why not now?"

"Because we have some champagne to drink and a dinner to eat. I've gone to a lot of trouble to arrange all this for a special evening and we're going to enjoy it."

Clare leaned into him, reveling in the heat and strength of his male body against her own. "And then?"

He lifted her up in his arms and whirled around with her, a look of supreme joy on his face, blended with love. "And then we go home."

THE EDITOR'S CORNER

We are preparing to light five huge candles on our LOVESWEPT birthday cake next month. And, because we are celebrating this special anniversary, I've asked to take back the writing of the "Editor's Corner" to make a lot of special announcements.

You have a gala month to look forward to with wonderful books both in the LOVESWEPT line and in the Bantam Books general list. The historical Delaney trilogy is coming and will go on sale at the same time the LOVESWEPTs do. Here's what you have to anticipate.

THE DELANEYS, THE UNTAMED YEARS

Historical splendor of post-Civil War America.
Unforgettable characters who founded the Delaney Dynasty
Spellbinding adventure ablaze with passion.

COPPER FIRE
By Fayrene Preston
Set in the Colorado Territory, 1873, **COPPER FIRE** tells the story of the tenderhearted spitfire Brianne Delaney, whose search for her kidnapped twin brother leads her into the arms of a rugged, ruthless man.

WILD SILVER
By Iris Johansen
From Imperial Russia to the Mississippi delta, 1874, **WILD SILVER** follows the exquisite half-Apache outcast, Silver Delaney, who is held captive on a riverboat by its mysterious owner, a young and irresistible, fallen Russian prince.

GOLDEN FLAMES
By Kay Hooper
Moving from New York to the New Mexico/Arizona border, 1870, **GOLDEN FLAMES** trails Falcon Delaney, the broodingly handsome loner who's spent years tracing a stolen cache of Union gold. But now he turns his skills to tracking the secrets of the bewitching woman who has stolen his soul.

And, going on sale April 20, 1988, as part of Bantam's Grand Slam promotion you will see copies everywhere of the breathtaking and spine-tingling . . . **BRAZEN VIRTUE** by Nora Roberts.

The steamy summer streets of Washington are no match for the phone lines of Fantasy, Inc., where every man's dreams come true. The "hotline" works perfectly for its anonymous clients and the teachers and housewives who moonlight as call girls . . . until a brilliant madman plugs in with twisted passion. Introducing GRACE McCABE, a gorgeous bestselling mystery writer determined to trap her sister's killer, and ED JACKSON, the handsome and tenacious cop you first met in **SACRED SINS.**

(continued)

We have more thrilling news for you. We're going to run a fabulous, fun contest throughout our Fifth Year called the "Hometown Hunk Contest." We will reissue six marvelous LOVESWEPT's (by six marvelous authors, of course) that were first published in the early days. The titles and authors are:

IN A CLASS BY ITSELF by Sandra Brown

FOR THE LOVE OF SAMI by Fayrene Preston

C.J.'S FATE by Kay Hooper

THE LADY AND THE UNICORN by Iris Johansen

CHARADE by Joan Elliot Pickart

DARLING OBSTACLES by Barbara Boswell

In the backs of our June, July, and August LOVESWEPTs we will publish "cover notes" just like those we use here at Bantam to create covers. These notes will describe the heroine and hero, give a teaser on the plot, and suggest a scene from the book for the cover. Your part in the contest is to see if a great looking man in your own hometown fits our description and your ideas about what the hero of one of these books looks like. If so, you enter him in the contest (contest blanks will be in the books starting month-after-next, too), along with his picture. The "hometown hunk" who is selected will be the model for a new cover of the book! We hope you'll find absolutely great looking men who are just perfect for the covers of these six great LOVESWEPTs. We can't wait to start judging those pictures! Indeed, a dozen women in the company who've heard about the contest are just begging to help open the mail!

And now for our terrific romances next month!

She started it all with LOVESWEPT #1, **HEAVEN'S PRICE**—Sandra Brown. And, naturally, we asked Sandra to lead off our Fifth Birthday list. Now you can relish **ADAM'S FALL**, LOVESWEPT #252, the thrilling story that brings back two great characters from **FANTA C.** Heroine Lilah Mason is challenged like she's never been before when she encounters ADAM CAVANAUGH again. Adam's down, but not out, flat on his back—yet he and Lilah learn he can still fall!

And, now it is a great pleasure to introduce two talented writers making their debuts with LOVESWEPT.

First, we have Tami Hoag presenting us with **THE TROUBLE WITH J.J.**, LOVESWEPT #253. Here's all the humor and heartwarming romance of two great people—lovely Genna Hastings and devastating J.J. Hennessy. She's the adorable lady next door; he's her new neighbor with rippling muscles and mile-wide shoulders. A don't miss read, for sure!

Next, there's **THE GRAND FINALE**, LOVESWEPT #254, by Janet Evanovich. **THE GRAND FINALE** is riotously funny and in the opening chapter pizza tycoon Berry Knudsen literally falls for tall, dark, muscular Jake Sawyer. She didn't really mean to, but somehow she got a perfect view of the perfect man through

(continued)

his bedroom window! Jake doesn't have her arrested for peeping because he's having too much fun watching her squirm as she tries to explain herself!

HOLD ON TIGHT, LOVESWEPT #255, is Deborah Smith's second book for us. You'll remember that her first was a wonderful island fantasy. **HOLD ON TIGHT,** a very different but equally strong love story, shows Deborah's range. It's set in both a small Southern town, and the big city of Birmingham and features sophisticated Dinah Sheridan, a former beauty queen turned politician wooed by Rucker McClure, an irreverent best-selling journalist/author. As Deborah says "the teasing, provocative Rucker McClure is just about as sexy as a man can get!" We're sure that you won't want to let go of **HOLD ON TIGHT.**

Josh Long's men—and his lovely wife, Raven—are back to help out one of Kay Hooper's most devastatingly sexy heroes ever in **OUTLAW DEREK,** LOVESWEPT #256. A beguiling and beautiful woman wanders into the life of a longtime loner and sets him on fire with love. In the midst of danger, Derek Ross gentles the sweet spirit of Shannon Brown in one of Kay's most memorable and touching romances ever.

And last, but never, never least is our own Iris Johansen, who will return next August to celebrate *her* fifth anniversary as a published author. Iris has created for us a very special birthday present, **MAN FROM HALF MOON BAY,** LOVESWEPT #257. Surprise. Panic. Then desire like an electric shock filled Sara O'Rourke when she saw Jordan Bandor across the crowded room. For eighteen months she'd lived free of the man from the harsh, unforgiving Australian outback who'd swept her off her feet, then wrapped her in a seductive web of sensual pleasure that left no room for work or friends. And now these two passionate people must work out their relationship in an atmosphere of desperate danger!

We started LOVESWEPT in a marketplace full of romances. Some said we'd never last. But we've been here for five happy years because of *your* support. Thank you from the bottom of our hearts, and here's to five more wonderful years!

Carolyn Nichols

Carolyn Nichols
   Editor

LOVESWEPT
Bantam Books
666 Fifth Avenue
New York, NY 10103

The first Delaney trilogy

Heirs to a great dynasty, the Delaney brothers were united by blood, united by devotion to their rugged land . . . and known far and wide as

THE SHAMROCK TRINITY

Bantam's bestselling LOVESWEPT romance line built its reputation on quality and innovation. Now, a remarkable and unique event in romance publishing comes from the same source: THE SHAMROCK TRINITY, three daringly original novels written by three of the most successful women's romance writers today. Kay Hooper, Iris Johansen, and Fayrene Preston have created a trio of books that are dynamite love stories bursting with strong, fascinating male and female characters, deeply sensual love scenes, the humor for which LOVESWEPT is famous, and a deliciously fresh approach to romance writing.

THE SHAMROCK TRINITY—Burke, York, and Rafe: Powerful men . . . rakes and charmers . . . they needed only love to make their lives complete.

☐ RAFE, THE MAVERICK by Kay Hooper

Rafe Delaney was a heartbreaker whose ebony eyes held laughing devils and whose lilting voice could charm any lady—or any horse—until a stallion named Diablo left him in the dust. It took Maggie O'Riley to work her magic on the impossible horse . . . and on his bold owner. Maggie's grace and strength made Rafe yearn to share the raw beauty of his land with her, to teach her the exquisite pleasure of yielding to the heat inside her. Maggie was stirred by Rafe's passion, but would his reputation and her ambition keep their kindred spirits apart?   (21846 • $2.75)

LOVESWEPT

☐ *YORK, THE RENEGADE* by *Iris Johansen*

Some men were made to fight dragons, Sierra Smith thought when she first met York Delaney. The rebel brother had roamed the world for years before calling the rough mining town of Hell's Bluff home. Now, the spirited young woman who'd penetrated this renegade's paradise had awakened a savage and tender possessiveness in York: something he never expected to find in himself. Sierra had known loneliness and isolation too—enough to realize that York's restlessness had only to do with finding a place to belong. Could she convince him that love was such a place, that the refuge he'd always sought was in her arms?

(21847 • $2.75)

☐ *BURKE, THE KINGPIN* by *Fayrene Preston*

Cara Winston appeared as a fantasy, racing on horseback to catch the day's last light—her silver hair glistening, her dress the color of the Arizona sunset . . . and Burke Delaney wanted her. She was on his horse, on his land: she would have to belong to him too. But Cara was quicksilver, impossible to hold, a wild creature whose scent was midnight flowers and sweet grass. Burke had always taken what he wanted, by willing it or fighting for it; Cara cherished her freedom and refused to believe his love would last. Could he make her see he'd captured her to have and hold forever?

(21848 • $2.75)